'You took your blood
through a hole in the
face of the rescue work

'Shut up, you. How's
'She's fine.'

'No I'm not,' Tracey whined, 'I'm in a coma.'

There was an excited murmur behind the rescuer. He turned to face the cameras. 'The girl's in a coma. The teacher's fine.' He turned back to Edward. 'You stay where you are. We're going to bring in some more equipment.'

'What the bloody hell for? We're both okay and we can climb out.'

'The teacher's going delirious. We'll need some more equipment,' the rescuer shouted to his team.

A hydraulic scoop with a battery of computer-controlled sensors swung into the hole. With pinpoint accuracy it struck Edward squarely on the forehead and bulldozed him, unconscious, back into the basement. The rescuer sighed.

'Right,' he shouted. 'The teacher's taken quite a bad knock. Bring in the Resuscitation Unit.'

1998

William Osborne
and
Richard Turner

SPHERE BOOKS LIMITED

SPHERE BOOKS LTD

Published by the Penguin Group
27 Wrights Lane, London W8 5TZ, England
Viking Penguin Inc., 40 West 23rd Street, New York, New York 10010, USA
Penguin Books Australia Ltd, Ringwood, Victoria, Australia
Penguin Books Canada Ltd, 2801 John Street, Markham, Ontario, Canada L3R 1B4
Penguin Books (NZ) Ltd, 182–190 Wairau Road, Auckland 10, New Zealand

Penguin Books Ltd, Registered Offices: Harmondsworth, Middlesex, England

First published in Great Britain in 1988 by Sphere Books Ltd

Copyright © William Osborne and Richard Turner 1988

Printed and bound in Great Britain by
Richard Clay Ltd, Bungay, Suffolk
Filmset in Palatino

1

Crichton tore the paper from his old Remington Imperial, let out a bronchial roar, crushed the sheet into a ball and flung it into the deep drift that was forming in a corner by the wall.

This, the thirteenth chapter, was stretching Crichton's creative powers to breaking point. One hundred and seventy-five times he'd tossed the first page of it into the corner. But how could the world's greatest and only living biographer lend any drama to the bare facts? All he knew was that Drake Matterhorn had had a bath that morning, dictated a memo to his brother and had breakfast on the patio. In all his seventy-five years Crichton had never faced a greater challenge.

He still had that memo somewhere. Where was it? — Ah:

MEMO
BRAD — COLONIZE THE ENVIRONMENT — DRAKE

Now how could the takeover of a simple, two-bit, third world, tin-pot, has-been excuse for a country like the Environment be of the slightest biographical significance? Certainly it had once been a great and powerful nation. Admittedly it had once been Crichton's home.

He took a slug of Old AmJap straight from the bottle and shuddered. His fingers set down the bottle and twitched over the keys. His face bunched as nausea clawed up from his belly. He braced his shoulders. Sighing between clenched teeth, he began to type:

I DID IT ANYWAY

THE LIFE AND CONQUESTS OF DRAKE MATTERHORN

CHAPTER THIRTEEN – THE ENVIRONMENT TAKEOVER

Drake Matterhorn lay back in a jacuzzi of warm Perrier in the West Wing of GoldTops, private palace and World Headquarters for the AmJap Corporation in Pearl Harbor, Hawaii. Scanning a vast television screen on the ceiling, his thumb pumping the button of a remote control at a hundred channels per minute, he meditated. Suddenly the Great Man was shaken by a spasm.

The control panel, slippery with exotic oils, shot from his grasp and clattered across the marble floor, but Drake heard it not. His eyes bulged with the bulge of the inspired. A choir sang 'Jerusalem'. There on the screen in all its glory was the central shopping precinct of Milton Keynes. 'I want it!' gasped Drake, clutching his failing heart.

And thus, the new era shit shit f,iuesrghli

Crichton drained the bottle of Old AmJap and tossed it into the air. It fell to earth, he cared not where.

2

The bombings that had punctuated life in the Environment since the middle of January nineteen ninety-eight were random and sporadic. Statistically, the chances of getting hurt were close to zero and did nothing to inhibit social activity. If anything, the bombings added a bit of spice, because to be near a bombing meant free television publicity. Anyway, what was there to worry about when all the bombed buildings were being replaced for free by a mystery foreign philanthropist billionaire?

Hyde Park had always been a popular arena for the promotion of trendy lifestyles. It was here that spring and the chance of a bombing had brought out some of London's most exotic flowerings. Among them, a council of Roman Elders, complete with togas, had set up a forum on the old bandstand — watched mournfully by some Early Christians, who squatted munching their Locust'n'Honey bars (with special additives for that faraway look) and admiring each others' rags. Another group of Romans, the leather type, was marching on Regent's Park to get some lions.

Scattered across the park and throughout London were neopunks, neolithic nomads, nudists, samurai warriors, *sans-culottes*, satanists, Trekkies, Marie Antionette shepherdesses, pearly kings and queens, beachboys, cowboys, indians, villeins, Tarzans, Knights of the Round Table, Visigoths and Care Bears. Bloodcurdling battle-cries, religious chants and primal grunts mingled with the strains of the troubadour's lute and massed renditions of the Smurf song.

Edward Wilson was taking a short cut to the Megamarket and was late. He was carrying his fetcher over Rotten Row as its little wheels couldn't cope with the deep ruts that the Seventh Cavalry had just made in the dirt.

'Edward. I think Laetitia's mad,' the fetcher squeaked.

'My girlfriend? She can't be,' Edward said.

'So why'd she throw kitchen appliances at you last night?'

'It was a row.'

'She said some pretty terrible things.'

'The truth never hurt anyone.'

'I bet it hurt when she threw the fridge at you.'

'I bet it hurt the fridge more than it hurt me.'

'I bet you have another row buying the new one.'

'We will if we're late.'

Edward and his fetcher set off along the path and watched the circus that milled around them. Edward was a morose, indecisive figure in his early thirties who hadn't found a lifestyle yet.

Since the Difficulties and the winding up of the Department, the whole Environment had become a scene of blissful chaos. Given the freedom to pursue their own fantasies, no-one could think of anything better to do than live out the exotic lives that had been idealized in popular art for over a century. No genre of literature, television or film was left unplundered as a source of inspiration. The plethora of new organizations that formed, advertised, recruited and initiated novices grew with every day. Every educational aid available to modern science was exploited: videos, pamphlets, courses, weekend try-outs, abduction, database mailing lists, extortion, seduction, news management, PR, special offers, film seasons, theme parks, computer games and fashion. Specialists in these media were themselves the greatest and most influential of all the stylists.

There was no longer any work or play – only a synthesis of both. Work was playing cowboys and indians (or doctors and nurses or cops and robbers or shopkeepers and customers) and was played like tribal warfare. The energy which was released by lawlessness of this marketing jungle had made the Environment into a hothouse of social creativity and the envy of the free world. Democratic principles had allowed the lunatics to take over the asylum. Majority rule at last.

Edward set the fetcher back on its wheels. On either side of the path, plastic daffodils peeped out of the hoar frost. It was the first day of spring, and that was official. Ahead, a crowd was forming. Half a mile beyond was the Megamarket.

There was a dull, distant boom and a faint tinkling of splintered glass. 'Yah! Missed us!' the fetcher squealed.

Edward scowled ahead. The crowd was forming a human log-jam against the exit to the Megamarket where a team of mediafreaks was cordoning off an area of grass and trees. A cordon usually meant that a telegenic event had been arranged, a chance for getting into shot – stardom, if only for a minute. No-one could resist it.

No-one except Edward. For him the crowd meant delay, delay meant annoying Laetitia and annoying Laetitia was becoming a habit. He hoisted the fetcher under his arm and ran.

Edward's run started a stampede. Using the fetcher as a battering ram, he barged through the wall of swaying backs as far as the cordon.

Arc-lamps, a loose circle of trucks and a network of fat, black cables provided the stage for a dead cert television spectacular.

'Cor!' said the fetcher.

'Oi! Stop pushing!' said a pale, overgrown youth with a stuffed bird of prey on his head.

'Sorry. What's going on?'

'Dunno, mate. What are you?'

'Pardon?'

'You got no chance, mate. Today, I, Ramses the Second, Son of Amon, King of Upper and Lower Nile, half man, half god, shall rise to ascendancy. My greater Presence will surely strike a big impression and get me on the telly. Kinn*ell!*'

A silver helicopter thundered low over their heads. The crowd roared and writhed as the glittering craft settled on the grass. There was an expectant hush as the rotors swished to a standstill. Two men in golden boilersuits and scarlet ear-protectors rushed a flight of carpeted steps to the side of the helicopter. The hatch opened.

Through the hatch wobbled two enormous, pink bosoms. Behind them was a short, red-headed girl with an angelic grin of such artless stupidity that it surpassed all fantasy. A moan rose from the mob. Today they had been truly blessed. They were in the presence of Tabafa Minx.

3

Isaiah Lunk moved with the grace and cunning of the animal after which he had been named: the Leopard. It was a name to be proud of. That name raised Isaiah Lunk above all men — all except one.

He sank his teeth into the belly of a hedgehog he'd saved over from breakfast, spat the entrails against the raw bark of a twisted hawthorn and read the signs. He was getting warmer. The gizzards had been telling him for days. His path was true and straight. His course was set. His keen instincts would guide him to the Different One. The Vision had come every night for over a week. It was a vision of a naked man with dreaming eyes. This man held aloft his right hand. The hand bore a bloody stigma. The man would cleanse himself and reappear dressed in green. Lunk knew that he had to find this man. How many of those shambling lumps of meat that call themselves human could say they had a mission as worthy as Lunk's? No-one took his lifestyle as seriously as him.

In the long, dark days of his childhood his kind father had taught him well. By keeping him locked for thirteen years under the stairs he had given his son time to think. Darkness became his friend and taught him wisdom. 'Thank you, Father, for you have given your son the gift of Vision,' said Lunk in a silent prayer to the man whom he released from the bonds of this earth with a hacksaw blade when the Voices told him his learning was complete.

Yet there was something in the way the lower bowel dripped, something in the attitude of the torn liver. For a week now, the entrails had been warning him of an increasing danger, a danger that exceeded all others. His mission was becoming more urgent. The orgy of silent slayings would lead him inexorably to the Different One — the Voices had told him as much — but when? *When?*

He tore the spiny skin from the hedgehog and chewed the meat meditatively.

4

Imagine you're the sort of person who thinks dumb, busty, submissive, young girls with sweet faces and no clothes are the feminine ideal. Hold in your mind's eye your most beautiful version of that girl. Now imagine that the girl you first thought of was only a Mark One prototype. What you're looking at now is the Mark Ten. Imagine how an erotomaniac cartoonist would draw this girl. That's what Tabafa Minx looked like.

'Who's that?' Edward asked.

Pharoah Ramses The Great turned in disbelief. 'You what? Thas' the Environment's top pin-up! Tabby! My Neffertitty! I come, O Queen!'

The Boy King ducked under the tape, charged towards his Destiny and was squashed into the mud by two security guards. The mob, irrespective of their lifestyles and creeds, wolf-whistled, jostled, cheered and jeered:

'WORRRR!'

'AAAAAHHHH!'

and

'GERREMOFF!'

Edward wondered at that. Apart from half a dozen sequins, the eighteen-year-old goddess was stark naked.

Reserve guards with riot shields sprang from the trucks as the baying and cat-calls intensified. Tabafa gurgled with delight, her baby grin widening as she waved to her subjects. She hopped from foot to foot under the arc-lamps, her prodigious bosoms bouncing in syncopation.

'Poor girl,' Edward thought aloud, 'she can't know how they're using her.'

'She doesn't,' said Ramses the Second, his eyes wide with excitement. 'That's her appeal. She's innocent. Still. It's only a bit of fun. Takes yer mind off all them bombings.'

'Perhaps that's the idea.'

'That's a bit perlitical, isn't it?'

'Aren't you ashamed to be standing ogling that poor girl?'

'What red-blooded man wouldn't?' said Ramses.

'Wouldn't be ashamed, or wouldn't ogle?'

'Both.'

'Well, my interest in women isn't restricted to slavering over naked teenagers.'

'Oh, I geddit. You was just strolling round looking for a chess partner when you accidentally pushed your way to the front, is that it?'

'Oh, for God's sake, let me through! Come on, fetcher.'

Edward held up the tape to let the fetcher trundle underneath and strode, head down, towards the park gate.

'Oi, you!'

He looked up. One of the mediafreaks was barking into a megaphone.

'Yeah, you!'

Heads turned.

'Who, me?'

'Yes, *you*. Don't move! Tab, lovey. Go drape yourself over that.'

Edward stood paralysed as the quintessence of nudity bobbed towards him under a forest of red hair. Saucer-like eyes of iridescent turquoise boggled into his own. A wave of vertigo washed over him. 'Er, hallo,' he said.

The metallic voice cut the air. 'Bit closer please, lovey!'

Tabafa draped one leg up the small of his back and nuzzled his shoulder-blade with her big toe. Laying her index finger to her plump lower lip, she pouted at the camera with the innocence of a ten-year-old. Cheeky Cherub. Edward had

14

seen her do that pose before on Channel Twenty-Four News.

'You! Smile!' barked the megaphone. Edward flexed the necessary muscles.

'Sorry 'bout him,' Tabafa said, switching pose from Cheeky Cherub to Venomous Vixen yet maintaining the sweetness of her voice. 'Still. 'S a lark, innit? Takes yer mind off all them bombings.'

'Um. These bombings seem to be getting a lot worse recently, don't you think?'

'Dunno, really,' she shrugged. ''Ere, d'you want an autographed picture?'

'No. No, really. Thank you.'

'Nah. Go on. Spoil yerself. Me Dad's got piles of 'em in the back of 'is Roller.'

A squat brute of a man in a camel coat heaved his way through the herd waving a sheaf of photographs over his fat head. Over his shoulder was a leather bus conductor's bag. He shook it to jingle the loose change. 'Come and get yer tasty pics of my little Tab! Saucy snapshots! Cheeky poses! She's a lovely bit of crumpet!' He leered at Tabafa and winked. Tabafa giggled and blew a kiss. Dad held out the photographs and submerged into the throng.

'Poor Dad. He works really hard for me,' Tabafa sighed, swapping Venomous Vixen for Novice Nun without even blinking.

'I suppose you must pay him well?' Edward asked.

'Oh, no. It's better than that. He pays *me*. I get an allowance – well, I do when 'is investments are goin' awright.'

'Just smile. If you can,' the megaphone man drawled. 'Okay. Ready! Now the kiss, Tab, please!'

A prurient chorus of 'Wooeurrgh!' heralded the event. Ample, red lips puckered towards Edward's. Curving the length of her body against him, she landed a long, wet kiss.

Standing with his arms limp, his face vacant of expression,

15

Edward was suddenly aware that Tabafa had gone and the crowd was already dispersing. 'Right. Megamarket. Come on, fetcher,' he said, staring towards the gate. 'Let's hope Laetitia's not cross.'

5

Sunlight burst gloriously over the tropical island paradise that was GoldTops. Sun-up is the time of day when Drake Matterhorn's vast palace was built to be seen. The solid gold roof that gives the AmJap Headquarters its name became a dazzling display of the world's most expensive sunlight. Piercing, twenty-two-carat rays were scattered into the swimming pool, across the rolling lawns, to every corner of the extensive, pampered grounds and out beyond the electric fence.

They also darted in thin shafts through some blinds that shielded a small window on the top floor of the East Wing. The light slatted harshly across a dozen empty bottles of Old AmJap gin, several thousand scattered cigarette ends and a hillock of white paper balls.

In the shadows, on a frail folding bed, under a filthy army greatcoat, Ashley Crichton, the world's greatest living author, was asleep, his grey, toothless jowls flapping wetly.

A crisp, white sheet of A4 was peeping from the roller of Crichton's faithful old Remington Imperial typewriter that stood on the card-table by the wall. It read as follows:

Draft 367

I DID IT ANYWAY
THE LIFE AND CONQUESTS OF DRAKE MATTERHORN
CHAPTER THIRTEEN — THE ENVIRONMENT TAKEOVER

Drake Matterhorn, the greatest man who ever lived, meditated deeply on his life's great achievements as he lay in his custom-built Barcalounger with electronic posture control and genuine leopardskin upholstery in the great ballroom of GoldTops. His family was grouped around him. Raiko, his latest and perhaps most beautiful wife yet, gazed at him adoringly. The eight-year-old twins, Jay, his son and heir, and Natalie, his enchanting daughter, were tugging open the presents brought to them by their Uncle Brad, Drake's devoted younger brother, who always gave them a thoughtful token on their birthday. Brad had spent much of his time in recent weeks far away in the West Wing Communications Centre executing Drake's orders for the efficient expansion of the AmJap Empire.

Brad watched proudly as Natalie carved her initials on her gold brick and Jay dashed outside with Brown, the faithful family retainer, to ram his key into the ignition of a Lagonda that waited on the drive. Drake beckoned to his brother.

'How's the Environment, Brad?'

'Five hits a day, Drake.'

'Go take it.'

'Yessir!'

And thus the new era oh god oh god oh go

Let's leave Crichton to his well-deserved rest. Things were happening in the palace grounds which he would have to add to the biography some other time.

6

The Great Wall of China and the Matterhorn family swimming pool are the only two man-made structures on the planet large enough to be seen from space with the naked eye. The still, blue waters of this chlorinated lake conceal a secret: the Matterhorn family rocket launchpad.

Brad Matterhorn stood on the launch gantry in his beige-and-cream crushed-velvet designer space suit. Brown stood by the open hatch of the Command Module holding a silver salver. On it sat a beige-and-cream crushed-velvet designer space helmet. Brown was nervously glancing at his watch. 'I think one would find it expedient, sir, to er prepare for lift-off. We have Tee minus three minutes and counting.'

'Hang loose, Brown. I know there's something I've forgotten.'

'I have taken the liberty of packing your golf-clubs, sir, and Cook has organized a hamper. You'll find it in the Service Module.'

'No no no. It's something vitally important. Damn! I remember. I forgot to buy the twins something expensive for their birthday. I *knew* there was something.'

The roar of liquid oxygen pumps and the hiss of freezing gas clouds billowing into the vast launch chamber echoed deafeningly. The tannoy announced above the din that unauthorized personnel had entered the Restricted Zone. Brad's electric-blue eyes blazed. 'You know, Brown, I love danger, don't you?'

'Danger and I are complete strangers, sir. We prefer to maintain a respectful distance. Tee minus two minutes and thirty seconds, sir.'

'I'm doing this for the Corporation, Brown. AmJap is my life. I'd pull my own head off for AmJap, wouldn't you?'

'Indubitably, sir.'

'Well, *I* would even if you wouldn't.'

'Might I be as bold, sir as to enquire of the purpose of this particular mission?'

'Gotta beef up the Environment takeover for Drake. He wants it bad.'

'Ah, the Environment,' Brown sighed wistfully.

'You know it?'

'The Old Country, sir. To me it's still home, even after all these years. I'm an Old Etonian, you know.'

'You surprise me, Brown. You speak English very well. What's it like?'

'An enchanted isle, sir. Little Indian corner shops, twenty-four-hour snooker, those little orange cones on the motor-ways . . .'

'Cut the crap.'

'Yessir. Tee minus two minutes, sir. And counting.'

The clatter of heavy feet marked the arrival of the twins. 'Uncle Brad! Uncle Brad! Don't go! We love you Uncle Brad!' They swarmed around him and clutched his knees.

'Please don't go, Uncle Brad!'

'Gee, I'm sorry, kids. You know your uncle loves ya,' he chuckled, patting their heads.

'Oh, yeah?' Jay challenged. 'So how come you forgot it was our birthday?'

'I think,' said Brown, 'that the children's birthday was yester-day, sir,'

'Brown. These are the most beautiful children in the world. If they wanna birthday every day of the year, that's their privilege and my honour.'

'Certainly, sir.'

'How many rockets do we have on the spare pad?'

'Three, sir.'

'Jay, how would you like your very own rocket?'

'Wowie!'

'It's yours,' said Brad, displaying his perfect dentition. 'Happy birthday.' He became suddenly grave. 'Now, Jay, Natalie. I have something very important to explain to you. Your Uncle Brad has to go to Yurp.'

The twins gasped in horror. 'Yurp!? Isn't that dangerous?' said Natalie.

'Tee minus one minute, sir. We have Launch Commit.'

'Sure it is, honey. But I have to go because of one little word. And that word is Doody. We all have to do our Doody.'

The twins hurled themselves about in hysterical laughter.

'What did I say, Brown?'

'I think the children may have found some childish ambiguity in your choice of words, sir. Will that be all?'

'Doody! Doody! Uncle Brad's gonna do a Doody on Yurp!' they chanted excitedly.

'Jay, Natalie. You have to go now. It's dangerous here.'

'Whaddabout Brown? How come he can stay?' Natalie asked.

'Yeah!' Jay added.

'You are my beloved niece and nephew. Brown is, is . . . what's the word, Brown?'

'Expendable, sir?'

'That's it. Expendable. Thank you, Brown. I don't know what I'd do without you. Now, scoot, kids!'

Brad snatched his helmet and ducked into the capsule. Brown slammed the hatch and fled. Inside, Brad set his jaw against the seven G's that were about to hit it. With the hydraulic hiss of the four billion horsepower needed to move the geographical feature that was the Matterhorn swimming pool, the sky opened up above. Brad glanced through the porthole to watch it. A tiny, pink fist was hammering against the glass.

'Uncle Brad! Uncle Brad! Whaddabout *my* birthday?'

'Natalie! Get away from here! I'll get you something from

the Environment!' he bellowed, veins bulging through his crew-cut. 'Now scoot!'

'Something expensive?'

'Sure, honey. Scram!'

The gantry trembled as Natalie scrammed and the engines rumbled.

'Gee, I love those kids,' Brad said as his chest took the full force of the acceleration. 'I'm gonna do it for them.'

7

'No, Edward. I'm not cross.'

'You sure?'

'Just shut up, will you?' Laetitia snapped. 'We're here to buy a fridge, not discuss my state of mind.'

'I told you she'd be cross,' said the fetcher.

'And why does that cretinous little monster have to come with you everywhere?'

'Can't get rid of him, really,' said the fetcher. Edward gave it a sharp sidekick. Laetitia turned away and cupped her face in her hands. Her shoulders began to twitch up and down. Edward looked across the scene of desolation that surrounded them. The Megamarket had been the epicentre of yet another bombing, which had partially destroyed a whole acre of the Homeware Section. The lifts were out of action, only the emergency lights were on and the main entrance hall was sprawling with new teams fighting over the best bits of debris.

'I'm sorry. It's not my fault,' Edward said.

'Oh, isn't it?'

'I got held up. And if I find out who let that bomb off I promise to punish the culprit severely.' He tried a playful prod in the ribs. 'Okay. Let's go to the Fridge Department,' he said.

'This *was* the Fridge Department,' Laetitia sobbed.

'Can't see any fridges . . .'

She built up a deathlook and whirled it on him. 'No. It's been restyled, you idiot! Can't you see? Post Holocaust. It's all the rage!'

'Really? Bit drastic. Looks like a bomb's hit it. Joke! . . . Joke!'

A cloud of Aramis wafted towards them. It contained a tall,

lean salesman with flared nostrils and a Pierre Cardin suit. 'Ah,' he said, inspecting Edward regally. 'The wanderer returns. Madame and I were beginning to despair.' He simpered at Laetitia.

'I got held up,' Edward explained flatly.

'Evidently. I do apologize for the inconvenience. Still, a good bombing takes one's mind off all those topless girls, I suppose.'

Edward coughed lightly. 'We'd like a fridge, please,' he said. The salesman turned.

'Any particular model?'

'I don't know. What do you suggest?'

He conducted a survey of Edward's plain shirt, baggy corduroys and scuffed shoes. 'Something simple?' he suggested.

'The simpler the better,' Edward said, glowering.

'I think I have the very thing for sir and madame,' the salesman said, turning to Laetitia. 'Amish!'

'Pardon?' she said.

'Really, madame,' he sighed, 'one is surprised one hasn't heard. It's the latest fashion. Everyone's into it. Seventeenth-century religious fundamentalism is the issue at stake here.'

'Oh,' said Edward. 'We are talking about a fridge, aren't we? I only ask because –'

'The Amish lifestyle does incorporate fridges, yes. In this case a *magnificent* fridge. Prepare yourselves. This is it . . .' He raised an arm and snapped his fingers. A powerful beam of white light fell vertically in front of him. A trumpet fanfare sounded as a platform floated down the beam and settled on the carpet. On the platform, in a blaze of light, stood a huge earthenware bell jar in a cast-iron bowl. Laetitia gasped.

'There,' said the salesman. 'Stands one full metre high, oatmeal finish, top-loading, 100% earthenware. No ice-maker, no crisper, no egg-rack. Just add water. It's the technological counter-revolution.' He tapped the top wih his knuckles. It rang hollowly.

'Looks like a clay pot in a trough to me,' said the fetcher.

'Yes. Beautiful, isn't it?' said the salesman.

Accustomed to user-friendly household appliances, the fetcher tried to engage it in conversation.

'Quite a novelty, isn't it?' the salesman simpered as the fetcher whizzed round and round the fridge in confusion. 'Kitchen Appliance at its most laconic. Free delivery and a year's warranty. Well, sir?'

'Erm . . .'

Laetitia's mouth dropped open. 'The latest —?'

'Oh, yes,' the salesman beamed, turning to Edward. 'Well?' Laetitia leaned round the salesman and nodded uncertainly.

'Yes, alright,' said Edward, producing his cashcard. The salesman snatched it into his pocket register, which blipped, said 'thank you' and regurgitated it.

'Right,' said Edward, stuffing the card back into his pocket. 'Shall we go?'

'No no no no no no no no no no no no no, sir,' the salesman said. 'We've only just begun. Come with me . . .' He swept them through an oaken door that opened into a dark side-room.

8

The AmJap Environment Headquarters building, standing a mile tall in the middle of the Thames, dominates the whole of London. Each side is made of a single sheet of reflective glass. Colonel Brad Matterhorn glanced down at the Environment's capital from the five hundredth floor. 'Jeez, what a dump,' he spat. His half-hour space flight and ten minute drive across London had told him that his tour in the Environment was going to be an arduous doody. The airport had been a nightmare. The customs officials seemed to be playing at their work and had held him up for a full minute. 'Twang. These guys had better shape up to AmJap efficiency or ship out,' he snapped.

'Waah, they don' unnerstan' nothin', sir,' Lieutenant Twang explained, his lazy Tennessee drawl adding at least five extra syllables to every word. 'We sure are glad to have you with us. This heyur's th'Operation Cenner, sir.'

Brad's steel-tipped boots tapped to a halt at a shining silver door.

'Please state your identity,' said the door.

'Waah, this heyur's Colonel Brad Matterhorn, who's takin' over as frum today. An', hell, you know me.'

The doors swished open to reveal a cavernous control room. Hundreds of uniformed staff were monitoring banks of VDUs. A cycloramic map of the Environment covered a whole wall. It was peppered with strange symbols that moved imperceptibly and changed colour without warning. A low electric hum pervaded the air. Brad inhaled deeply and closed his eyes to savour the sheer power. It tasted good. 'You're flabby, Twang!' he exploded.

'Sir?'

'Flabby! Look at my body! I have muscle tone, Twang. Feel those muscles.' Twang prodded a biceps. It might have been granite. 'That is an AmJap body. But your body is not an AmJap body. It is a flabby body. It is made of flab. I hate flab. I hate the very word. Listen to it. I'm gonna say it once more, much as it disturbs me. Fla-bee! Shape up, Twang.'

'Yessir!' Twang saluted and held himself rigid. Brad snatched a tiny bottle from the top zipper in his suit and thrust it on to Twang's chest.

'Take these. Latest from the R and D boys in Pearl Harbor.' Twang took the bottle and eyed it.

'Before or after meals, sir?'

'*Instead* of meals.'

'Sir.'

'Well?'

'Sir?'

'When's the next hit?'

'Our two best destruction agents are waiting to address you on that matter, sir. Shall I call them in?'

Brad nodded imperially.

'CL! Bushido!'

In an instant, two of the uniformed staff were saluting Brad in perfect military formation. CL, a blonde Amazon with broad shoulders and high cheek bones, stood a foot taller than Bushido, an athletic-looking Japanese male whose face made a serious point of expressing precisely nothing.

Brad encircled them. The two destruction agents continued to face front without blinking. These were AmJap bodies with AmJap minds.

'CL 'n' Bushido, sir. Toove ayer fahniss.'

'Pardon me?'

'Ah say this heyur's CL 'n' Bushido. Two of our fahnest men – 'cep one's a woman. 'Speck you noticed, sir.'

27

'Which one's CL and which one's Bushido?'

Twang shrugged his shoulders. Brad looked to the female.

'Well?'

'That's classified, sir,' she said in a flat, rich baritone.

Brad squared himself to address them. 'Your next hit will be your first under my command.'

'Sir!' they barked as one.

'Where's it gonna be?' Brad demanded.

'Our next hit is the Baby Burger Bar in Rei-cester Square at twelve hundred hours tomorrow. Sir!' said the Japanese.

'Make it neat, make it punctual, but above all, make it beautiful! Dismiss!'

With mechanical precision the destruction agents dismissed.

9

They stood face to face. There was nowhere to sit. 'Oh, yes,' Edward began. 'You certainly bloody fell for it this time, didn't you? That salesman had you eating out of the palm of his hand. Who's idea was it to come home on a donkey cart dressed as seventeenth-century peasants just to impress the neighbours?' He stabbed a finger at her.

'If you knew I was making a mistake, why didn't you stop me?'

'Ha bloody ha. Me and who's team of wild bloody horses?'

'There's no need to swear, Edward. I had no idea the flat would end up looking like this.'

'I remember exactly what you said at the time, *actually*. And that smarmy git had my cashcard off me before I could say Robert Robinson.'

'"No" would have been more appropriate.'

'Letty, I had no idea buying a simple fridge meant a gang of men would bring us back from the Megamarket, rip out the appliances and turn the place into a seventeenth-century hovel, and neither did you.'

'I want you to go back right now and demand a complete refit. Look at the place.'

Edward looked about. He kicked at the straw on the uneven earth floor. 'Have some henbane or something, Letty. It'll calm you down,' he said, uncovering a heavy trunk marked 'Herbale Remydyes' and opening the lid. 'Fetcher. Draw a bucket of water from the well, would you?'

He offered her a stoppered, green bottle. Laetitia took it and tossed it aside. The fetcher ground and whirred towards a

29

heavy wooden lid on the rough floor. It lifted the lid and teetered dangerously on the lip of the well.

Laetitia folded her arms across her black, hessian frock. 'Either you return this house to the twentieth century or I'm going,' she said.

'Look,' Edward said. 'How about some supper? I'll soon get the stove going. What's in the fridge? He tilted the earthenware bell jar to one side and peered into the murky water in the cast-iron bowl. Balancing the bell with one hand, he fished out two lettuce leaves. They hung like seaweed across his palm. Laetitia looked about to vomit.

'I hate you, I hate you, I hate you!' she screamed.

One of Laetitia's clogs cartwheeled over Edward's head and into the soft, clay wall. 'Edward . . .' the fetcher whined. 'Nothing'll talk to me.'

'Try the television,' Edward said as a second clog shot clean through a leaded window. 'At least they left that.'

'Television? Aw, you poor thing.' The fetcher rummaged along the wall to the one remaining power socket.

'I hate you!' Laetitia blubbed.

'That's it. Let it all come out,' Edward said.

'You and your mouth. "Something simple", you said. "The simpler the better"!' She prised a clog out of the wall, slipped it on and hopped to the hall, slamming the door heavily on its forged iron hinges. The fetcher gave a cheer as the television burst into life.

'Oh. Hello, fetcher. Himmel. Vere em I?'

'Television. Quick. Put the news on. They're having another row.'

'Jawohl!' The television executed a lightning flick through the channels. The lantern jaw of a breezy young presenter flashed into view.

'Hi there Environmental News main stories spring surprise in Hyde Park the Leopard kills again in the North another

Megamarket bomb causing millions of pounds worth of damage that's after the break!'

A string of adverts advertising advertising agencies, unheard-of style corporations and things to put in your hair spilled into the room in a torrent of disco funk, Vivaldi and a massed choir of happy investors.

Laetitia re-entered clutching a stuffed Smurf and a handful of knickers. 'I'm going to collect my linen, get the donkey out of the stable and go!' she announced, rifling the drawers of a heavy pine cabinet with more than necessary force.

'Oh, stay and watch the television.'

'I used to think you were an interesting individualist. I used to think you were going to *be* somebody, but now I know you're flabby-minded and stupid.'

'You're upset, aren't you?'

She stamped off through the straw. 'I loathe you!' she called back.

'Oh, come on. "Young Opticians" is on in five minutes. Your favourite.' Edward listened as the stable door creaked open and the donkey stomped into the hall. 'Come and watch the news and I'll pour you a flagon of mead.'

A minute later Edward was suppressing a smirk as Laetitia crept back in, fingering a knotted leather harness. He brushed some straw off the Herbale Remydyes trunk and sat down at one end. She sat down at the other, sniffing at the tangle in her lap.

'Welcome back,' said the presenter. 'I hope you're full of the joys of spring today because today's the day for all young lovers to forget their cares and gambol in the daisy-covered meadows and that seems to have been happening all over the Environment today, because today's the first day of spring.'

'That donkey's left a present in the hall, in case you're interested,' Laetitia said, smiling weakly.

'And that brings us to our main story Tabafa Minx top

Environment pin-up just couldn't resist a spontaneous frolic among the daffodils today and came busting out all over Hyde Park to the surprise and delight of our news team who managed to catch your favourite busty nymphette in a private moment of sheer exuberance.'

Edward put his arm around Laetitia's shoulder. 'Oooh! Oooh! It's springtime! Oooh! Oooh!' said Tabafa, gamboling across the grass and waving to her fans. Edward moved in for a kiss to the forehead.

'Look, Edward. It's you!' the fetcher squealed. Laetitia drew back sharply. On the television, Edward was in a clinch with the Environment's top pin-up.

'– and one fan just couldn't resist running up and grabbing a kiss from his favourite fantasy-girl – lucky fella!' said the announcer.

'Cor!! –' said the fetcher.

'Television! Off!' Edward screamed.

'– What huge, big bazoomas Tabafa's got!' the fetcher shrieked.

'Look, Laetitia. It's not what you think.'

Laetitia turned and left.

Edward stared at the fetcher for a full minute. 'You've really done it this time,' he said at last.

'Am I going to get a smack?' the fetcher asked.

'Yes.'

'Where shall I stand?'

'Just there.'

The fetcher trundled to the spot. Edward delivered three brutally cold-blooded kicks. 'Ow. Ow. Ow,' it said, retracting its domed head.

'Television!'

'Edvard! I vos only obeying orders!'

'Shut up and show me something cheerful.'

'Vot about ze Lonely Hearts Chennel?'

Edward shrugged. 'Okeydoke.'

32

A bony female in the full lotus position burst on to the screen. 'Hi. I'm Marylou. My hair's natural, my teeth cost my dad a fortune, I work out regular and my therapist says I'm nearly there. So you're wondering why I need to advertise for a soulmate? Haha. Are you tall, multi-talented, decisive, dynamic, successful, supportive, stylish and a Leo?'

'Bugger. I think I'm a Taurus.'

'Taurus? Switch me over. I'm wasting my time,' she drawled as her image fizzled away.

'Okay, television. That's enough. Fetcher.'

'I'm not talking to you,' the fetcher said from inside its plastic casing.

'Yes you are.'

'You always win that argument.'

'God, life is bloody boring,' said Edward. 'I suppose I'd better find something vaguely interesting to do until another girlfried turns up. Television. Show me the professional pastimes vacancies channel.'

10

'Teaching's more than a professional pastime. It's a whole lifestyle,' wheezed Claire, the overweight, menopausal head teacher, as she laboured up a long staircase in the Battersea Centre for Infant Development. 'In six months I've grown to love it. I'm sure you'll be fine. We're none of us born teachers, but you'll soon get the hang of it if you decide to take it up.'

'Well, there's no harm in having a look round,' Edward shrugged.

'Lovely dear. Duck.' She wrestled him on to the lino with surprising agility as two patches of graffitoed plaster exploded from the corridor wall above them.

'What was that?'

'Dumdum bullets,' she sighed. 'Little tinkers. That's against the Geneva Convention *and* they know it.' She helped Edward to stand. 'Decision-making for the under-fives, was it?'

'Well, obviously I haven't made my mind up yet . . .'

'Don't worry, Mr Wilson. The kids'll decide for you. They always do,' she assured him, patting him down the corridor and glancing down at the playground. 'Head down.'

They crouched below the window ledge. A heavy object crashed through the glass, left a nasty dent in the wall and came to rest on the floor.

'We must get through five video recorders a week that way,' she said, absently picking a sliver of glass from Edward's lapel. 'I don't know where they get the energy from.'

'The blue bits in the breakfast cereal.'

'Now this is Theresa's class,' she said, approaching a battered door. She turned the handle and listened. A thin voice trailed through the gap.

'Now. What we see here, class, is a reaction between two non-dichotomous social forces —'

'Marketing Science for the hyperactive,' Claire explained in a low whisper. She opened the door wider. The classroom contained no children.

'On the Y-axis we can see an exponential increase concomitant with a decrease on the —'

'Theresa, lovey, where's your class?'

'I've eaten them,' she said. Her hair hung in thin rats' tails around her gaunt, grey face. Behind her, the blackboard was covered with violent scrawlings. Her face twisted as her head rocked back and released a high, ghostly wail that echoed down the corridor. Claire hurried Edward away by the arm.

'She's only joking,' she said, biting her lip.

'Get down!' Edward shouted, pulling her bulk to the floor just in time. A crossbow bolt pronged into the wall above them. They weaved and zigzagged with their heads down towards the end of the corridor.

'We're getting the hang of it already, Mr Wilson,' she panted, passing an admiring glance. 'Now, in here we have decision-making for the five-and-unders. Let's go take a peek.'

Claire opened the door a crack and waved a white hanky through the gap. From the other side came the friendly babble of children's voices. She opened the door and pushed Edward in. The babble died to a murmur. 'Good morning, Decision-makers One,' said Claire.

'Good morning, Claire!' they chorused in return.

'Where's Mr Thomas?'

'Please, Claire,' said a girl at the back, raising an arm that jangled with cheap jewellery.

'This is Tracey,' said Claire. 'Underneath all that make-up. What is it, Tracey?'

'Please, miss. Who's that hunk with you?'

'My word!' said Claire. 'That's a very grown-up thing for a

35

five-year-old to say, now isn't it?' She beamed at Edward. 'I think they like you.'

Tracey leant her fist on her hip, which was accentuated by a tight rubber mini skirt. A pink bubble swelled from her scarlet lips. She sucked it back in, popped it, winked a mascara'd eye at Edward and tossed the blonde highlights of her permed hair. Edward gulped.

'Hello children. Erm. Where's Mr Thomas gone, then?' he asked.

Tracey sat on her desk and crossed her legs. Edward noticed that she was wearing suspenders. 'Well, erm. I'm sorry, I didn't quite get your name . . .?' she purred.

'Mr Wil –'

'This is Edward,' Claire interrupted.

'Well, Edward,' said Tracey, 'I think Mr Thomas has run away.' The class giggled.

'When?' said Edward.

'This morning,' said Tracey.

'Oh, loveys. He's *left* you,' Claire gushed. 'Now, don't feel deserted. You're still loved.' She gave Edward a pained look. 'Poor lambs. We must avoid a traumatization. Would you step in today? Would you do that for me?'

'Well, I – they seem alright,' Edward said, his eyes darting to the door.

'Yes. They do, don't they?' said Claire.

'Okay.'

'Did you hear that, class? Edward's come to the rescue. Well. Let's give him some motivational reinforcement, shall we?' Thirty infant larynxes shrieked in approval. 'See you in the staff room after!' Claire shouted as she shot down the corridor.

'Right. Right. Now then. Right. Erm. Decision-making for the five-and-unders. Right. Er. So. What I want us to – that is, er, I think it would be a jolly good idea if we all got down to discussing the subject of individual choice. So, let's talk about the decisions we all make every day of our lives, then. Erm.'

'Please, Edward. What did you do in the Difficulties?' said a sharp, little voice.

'Well, I —'

'Mr Thomas was a commando,' said another.

'Was he? Well. I —'

'*He* killed thirty people.'

'Did he really?'

'Are you the Leopard?'

'The Leopard's killed forty-three people,' another one added.

'Have you got a girlfriend?' Tracey asked.

'Yes. Well. No.'

'Ooooooh!' the class howled.

'I've seen you on the telly!' shouted a little nose-picker.

'Quiet, please. Now. Decisions. Supposing I had to make a choice, er —'

'Like buying something?'

'Yes, that's it. Like buying something,' Edward said, smiling. 'Buying something. Like —'

'A hamburger, Edward?'

'Alright. A hamburger. Now. I have a choice. I could have —'

'A quarterpounder?'

'Yes . . .'

'A Crunchyburger?'

'Very good. Anyone else?'

'A Whopper?'

'Very good, Tracey. Sit down.'

'Can I have a Mister Fizz and medium fries please, Edward?'

'I want a Cheese Quippledecker!'

'Please, Edward,' said Tracey. 'I've just had a really good idea . . .'

11

The corridors were silent. Not a single bullet or paving slab went near Edward on the way to the staff room. He hammered on the heavily armour-plated door. A barred shutter opened to reveal a deeply lined face. 'Hello? What do you want?' it said.

'Edward Wilson. Decision-makers One. Can I come in?'

'Oh. Absolutely, old chap,' the face said, breaking into a charming smile. Bolts were shot, chains released, double-mortise locks turned and combinations dialled. 'At the double, if I were you, old boy,' the man said, opening the door just far enough to let Edward in before slamming it and reversing the business with the locks. 'It's the poison darts I'm afraid of. A brick you can see. Phillips,' he said, extending a hand. 'Welcome aboard.'

'I need the keys for the school bus. I've got Decision-makers One waiting outside in it.'

'Shouldn't worry,' said Phillips. 'They'll have hot-wired it by now. No need to show them how an engine works, if that's the purpose of the exercise.'

'Oh, no. They've decided —' Edward corrected himself, '*I've* decided to go on a field trip to the Baby Burger Bar.'

Phillips put his arm round Edward's shoulder and breathed stale whisky over him. 'Been feeling depressed lately?'

'No. What makes you think —?'

'Thinking of ending it all?'

'*No*, I —' Phillips withdrew his arm, took a briar from the pocket of his Harris tweed, tapped it on the bottom of one of his brogues and looked pained.

'You've got me baffled, old stick. Care for a scotch? Valium?'

Edward followed Phillips to a loose circle of chairs. Phillips planted himself in a tattered leather armchair and began to light up. 'Got all the parents to sign legal release forms in triplicate, all that guff?'

'No. Tracey said —'

'Tracey?' Phillips exploded. 'It's worse than I thought! Take my advice, old sausage, and steer clear. That girl's a blister of the worst kind. Poison. You're way out of your depth.' He frowned into the bowl of his pipe and puffed agitatedly.

'But, you see I rather, sort of . . . promised them.'

'Bad luck old fruitcake,' Phillips said, rising and surveying the playground through the barred window. 'But I suppose lightning never strikes twice in the same place . . .'

'What?'

'Four months ago,' said Phillips, keeping his eye to the glass. 'North face of the Eiger. School hang-gliding trip. One of my class —'

'But this is only a trip to the Baby Burger Bar,' Edward protested.

'Don't see the difference, old squash.' He eyed the battle-scarred tarmac in silence. 'Look. If anything goes wrong, insist on a cell to yourself. The criminal fraternity doesn't take kindly to your sort.'

'A cell to —? What d'you mean, "my sort"?'

'The sort of person the papers'll *say* you are!' Phillips blurted, turning to face Edward. Tears were trickling down his cheeks. 'That's why I wear this rubber mask!' He dug trembling, nicotine-stained fingernails into his face and tore it off. Edward gaped in horror at the scarred and hideously deformed features underneath the latex. 'I was in Solitary, but they got to me in the end. Razor blades in the soap. Still,' he said, becoming suddenly brisk. 'Mustn't welsh on Decision-makers One — fate worse than death. You'd better cut along. Wouldn't want to be in your shoes, old man. Not for the world.'

He opened a metal cabinet on the wall, took out a key, dropped it into Edward's hand and bundled him towards the door. He unlocked it and shoved him out into the corridor. 'Keep your head down and weave!' he shouted, locking himself back in.

'I was only trying to keep the boy warm from the snow,' he murmured, staring into the bowl of his pipe.

12

'Hi,' said CL, pointing to the gothic lettering on the back of Bushido's overalls. 'We're from Ye Olde Environmente Plumbing Company. We got a call about, er, some problem with your plumbing. Can we check it out?'

'Certainly,' said the cash register.

'Thank you most kindly. Bushido, get the tools.'

'Why is it always me who has to carry the explosives?'

CL's eyes darted around the eating area. 'Shut up,' she hissed, 'you mean the *plumbing equipment*. Because, Bushido, I outrank you, that's why.'

'Oh, yeah,' said Bushido, 'What rank are you?'

'That's classified. Not even *I* know. Now git!'

'Git this, git that,' Bushido muttered, strolling out to the van.

CL stood at the counter and watched as a typical Environment family approached to make their orders. 'Awright, Wayne,' the father said, 'I'll get you one.'

'Aw, Dad,' the kid whined, 'I want two! I want two! I want two! I want two! I want two! I want two! I want two!'

'Shuddup Wayne,' the father said, cuffing him wearily. 'Bloody kids.'

The mother had pinioned a younger son against a concrete pillar and was trying to wipe snot from his face. 'AAAAAAAAAGHGHGHGHGHGHGH!' said the child.

'Awright Darren. Good boy.'

'AAAAAAAAAGHGHGHGHGHGHGH!'

'Darren shut his gob and Mummy buy Darren a Mr Badgerburger.'

41

'AAAAAAAAAG–' CL squeezed a pressure-point on the child's head.

'Er. Pordon moi, mite. Could yew an' yer famly ploise stand asoide?' she said in Dick van Dyke cockney.

'Whas goin' on, then?' the father asked, ambling up with a Baby Burger hat on his head and hugging a dustbin-sized milk shake.

'Ha! Merely a minor plumbing malfunction, good sir,' CL said, rapping her kunckles on the pillar. 'Service! Excuse me! Excuse me! Chop! Chop! Hello! Shop!'

'How can I help you?' the cash register replied. CL pointed at the pillar.

'This the main support pillar?'

'Yes.'

'Good. Seems to be where the problem is.'

'Here you are, CL' said Bushido, dropping a bag at CL's feet. 'Found a good spot?'

'Yeah. Runs straight up to the stanchion. Should bring down the whole kerboodle like a deck of cards.' Bushido spat into his hands and rubbed them together.

'Hey, shop! Got a point for my drill?'

'It's behind you,' the cash register replied.

Bushido drilled into the masonry while CL wired the charge to the timer. The man in the Baby Burger hat watched with his mouth hanging open. 'What is it, then? Drains?' he asked.

'Sure. Why not?' said CL. 'Get outta here, willya?'

''Ere, Dad. Dad. Dad. Dad! *Dad!* Da-a-a-d!!' Wayne cried, pointing at the lump of gelignite that CL was preparing. 'That looks tastier than what I've got.'

'Aw, come on, Wayne,' the father said, dragging Wayne away by the ear. 'Get out the way. These people are busy.'

The automatic glass doors opened. Edward stood in the entrance. A wave of children crashed over him and charged for the counter, cheering wildly and calling their orders. 'Now, don't run! Think before you choose!' he shouted, picking himself up from the ground. They milled around the counter, fighting for a place at the front and throwing the automatic cash register into confusion. The dispenser issued a torrent of junk food that was snatched away and fought over.

'That's it, Decision-makers! You'll soon get the hang of it! Think about what you want and then ask yourself why you think that's the right choice! Think carefully! Right. Now, when you've done that, find yourselves a seat, children,' Edward yelled over the tumult, leaning against a pillar.

'I'm sorry, sir,' said the tall woman in overalls. 'This area has been sealed off. For plumbing. Now, git!'

'What? Drains, is it?' said Edward, peering round the pillar to watch the squat Japanese drilling a hole on the other side.

'Okay. Ready for the jelly,' the Japanese said, withdrawing the bit and blowing dust away from the hole.

'What d'you want jelly for?' Edward asked. The tall blonde smiled.

'Oh. He's such a child,' she explained. 'In a *minute*, Bushido.'

'No,' Bushido bellowed without looking up. 'We gotta brow it now.'

'You've blown it now alright,' CL hissed, hooking a thumb at Edward.

'Blow what?' Edward asked. Bushido glowered at CL. 'I am an AmJap samurai. I never brow anything except up. You have impugned my honour.'

'Oh, no. Not that old chestnut,' CL groaned.

'You do not understand, do you? My mission is to brow up this building for AmJap. If I fail, I must commit *hara kiri*. For me, face is all that matters.'

'Ha! With *that* face? No wonder you're suicidal.' said CL. Edward looked at the wires, the jelly and the digital clock.

'Here. You're not bombers, are you?' he asked.

'No,' CL corrected. 'Plumbers.'

'Please, sir. Tracey's got locked in the loo downstairs and wants you to get her out.'

43

'Everyone get out! There's a bomb in here. Get out!' Edward shouted. A sea of infant panic gushed out through the doors. He glanced back at the pillar. The wires were connected and the plumbers were gone. 'My God!' he gasped, flying towards the stairs and down to the toilets. 'Tracey!'

His heart pounding, his feet scrambling with a will of their own, Edward heard Phillips' rueful voice echoing in his skull: 'Wouldn't want to be in your shoes, old man. Not for the world.'

Edward hammered on the lavatory door. 'Tracey! Come out! Come out now! There's a bomb in here!'

'I can't, Edward. I need a big strong man,' she replied.

'I'm telling you for the last time. Please come out.'

'You'll have to climb over and give me a *hand*, Edward.'

Edward slapped his hand on his forehead. He looked up at the top of the door, sighed and climbed over, landing heavily on the floor next to Tracey. His hands fumbled over the door. 'Where's the lock? Quickly!!'

'Guess.'

'You haven't heard the last of this,' said Edward.

'KERRRBOOOOOMMMMM'! went the Baby Burger Bar.

13

As Ye Olde Environmente Plumbing Company's van sped through the London traffic towards Westminster, Bushido looked back. 'Think that guy suspected anything?' he said.

'Even if he did, he'll never get out alive,' said CL. 'Let's just forget him and file our report.'

14

Laetitia luxuriated between Gordon's black, satin sheets and calculated his chances of keeping her happy. They were good. Gordon was a man of action, a man of style. Only half an hour before when his laserpager went off somewhere in the bed, he was on to his Cartier telephone within seconds. Within minutes he was up, immaculately dressed and out of the door on important business. 'Ciao, honey,' she murmured to herself, remembering the thrill of his parting words. Their very coolness sent ripples of pleasure up and down her spine.

Now, with the whole, snazzy flat to herself, she was able to explore his wardrobe and interrogate the kitchen appliances and other general gadgetry about the exact value of her new catch. But first a spot of telly for an update on the latest trends. 'Television?' she asked the bedroom at large.

A flatter, squarer screen than she ever thought possible emerged discreetly from the foot of the bed and turned casually to face her. 'Oh, hallo . . .' it said.

'News, please. Any channel.'

'Sure. Okay,' the screen said. 'Howzabout this?'

'Hi. It's one o'clock. News time, kids. Top people are watching TV Face, the exclusive cable service for the *jeunesse dorée* – are *you*? Main stories first . . . Tabafa Minx: is she the ideal girl she's cracked up to be? We wanted *your* opinion. And we got it. Survey results later on. Plus: the Leopard – more savage killings, this time even further south – exclusive, grisly pictures to follow. And we'll be asking: the Leopard – psychopath, trendsetter or both? Stick your finger in that dial and let us know. But first, over to Bazzer Bazalgette for the latest on the Baby Burger Bar tragedy. Bazzer.'

A man with a microphone splashed on to the screen. 'Thanks, Norm,' said Bazzer, his voice breathy with reverence. He was standing in somebody's living room. Behind him on the pink dralon sofa sat a couple in their late twenties. On the wall behind them was an enormous framed photograph of a pretty five-year-old girl in a white tutu.

'Little,' said Bazzer, 'if anything, now remains of the Baby Burger Bar, devastated, as we have all seen, by a mysterious bomb. There were only two people in the building at the time and they are thought to be trapped in the little girls' room in the basement area. They've been identified as Edward Wilson, the teacher responsible for the school outing, and five-year-old Tracey Wex, the cheerful, popular, brave little schoolgirl who has already stolen the hearts of millions. She's thought to be in a coma. Teams of journalists are right now in Leicester Square, waiting to make their verdict on the teacher, Edward Wilson. Is he the Pedagogue of Death, as some have dubbed him, or merely criminally negligent? And why was Wilson in the little girl's room in the first place?' Bazzer wheeled on his subjects. 'Mrs Wex. As Tracey's mother, just how devastated do you feel right now?' He held the microphone tenderly under her nose.

'Very bitter,' Mrs Wex sniffed. 'It's hit me like a wall.'

'Mrs Wex is crying real tears,' Bazzer exclaimed, pointing and beckoning the camera to close in.

'Don't worry, Betty,' the husband said, laying his arm across her plump shoulders and squinting at the autocue. 'Our Trace'll be alright.'

'Oh, Bert. I can't help it,' Betty said, taking a tissue from Bazzer and burying it in her face. 'Our Trace. Our little Tracey. Our one and only. I know it. She's going to – she's . . . going to be . . . famous!'

'*And* you, you bastard!' Laetitia screamed, clawing at the sheets and hurling a wine-glass, an alarm-clock and Gordon's 'Mister Men' posing pouch at the screen. '*And* you, Edward! You lucky, famous bastard! Oh, of all the miserable luck!'

15

Edward squatted on his haunches against a corner of the cramped cubicle and stared into space. Beside him, Tracey hummed herself a little tune and arranged her make-up. Fifteen feet above their heads, rival gangs of journalists and rescue workers were fighting each other for the recording rights to the dramatic rescue and scandalous exposé of the Pedagogue of Death. They had decided that the rescue would look more dramatic after nightfall, under lights, and at peak viewing time.

On the doorstep of her cosy little home in Dunstable, Mrs Violet Wigge was making her last, tearful farewells to her beloved lodger, Norbert Seriously, who had decided to become a hippy and go off on the road to Free Love and adventure. He was loaded down with hippy manuals, Mrs Wigge's sandwiches and three months' supply of clean underwear.

Back in London, the Environment's top pin-up was frowning. She had just read the latest opinion poll results and discovered that her popularity was down for the first time in her six-month career. She tossed back a handful of little pills, picked up her pink, funfur trimphone and punched her father's number.

On the top floor of the towering AmJap Environment headquarters building in the middle of the Thames, Colonel Brad Matterhorn brooded angrily over the classified reports of destruction agents CL and Bushido. 'Those guys screwed up,' he spat.

16

The moon draped a silvery, gossamer shroud over the East Wing of GoldTops, where Crichton dozed on the balcony outside his room. Hanging from his sleeping hand was a scrap of tear-stained paper — the latest version of Chapter Thirteen of *The Life and Conquests of Drake Matterhorn*. It was still missing an awful lot. It needed facts. For instance, what was the significance of the phone call just after midnight? What was so important that Brown had to wake the Master himself to answer it? According to Brown it was Brad on the line, and Brad didn't sound happy. Drake didn't look happy either, Brown said. He ground his teeth, said 'Go flat out, Brad. I want it in three weeks!' and slammed down the receiver. How could Crichton write without facts? Here's his attempt:

Draft 505

I DID IT ANYWAY
THE LIFE AND CONQUESTS OF
DRAKE MATTERHORN
CHAPTER THIRTEEN — THE ENVIRONMENT TAKEOVER

Drake Matterhorn loved the world so much and the Environment so particularly that he sent his only brother there to take it for him. Safe in the knowledge that Brad was a man of outstanding virtue, a man to get things done, Drake slept peacefully on his magnificent panda-skin bed (dreaming of AmJap perfection as it spread across the world, of the beginning of a millenium of peace and prosperity for humankind, of a future guaranteed by this final conquest) when he became faintly aware of a distant trilling on the very outer edge of his slumbering consciousness. It was the telephone. Drake clasped at the receiver and held it to his ear. It was a call from London. Bad news. What could possibly have gone wrong? How the hell do I know?

50

In the West Wing Communications Centre, Drake was unaware of the turmoil in the mind of his biographer. In fact, he was unaware of any biographer at all. He had hired Crichton on a passing whim. The whim had passed from his memory even before Crichton had left his home in Streatham Hill for Hawaii.

If Crichton had only known his true status, he could have enjoyed a life of luxury and abandon. He could have drunk, smoked, slept and written what he liked (pornography) without let or hindrance until his dying day. Only fear and ignorance forced him to continue his thankless work.

On the other side of GoldTops, in the West Wing, Drake Matterhorn was engrossed in war. Violent struggle – he loved it in all its forms. Best of all he loved it on television. On the enormous screen in one of the many reviewing lounges in the Communications Centre, he was monitoring a war he had recently commenced in a small South American country. AmJap-sponsored freedom fighters, equipped with AmJap technology, were unbeatable value. Using his remote control panel, Drake was able to direct troop movements, zoom in on the goriest details of satellite surveillance and occasionally flick over to watch the latest in the sixteenth series of *Dynasty*.

How Drake Matterhorn hated Blake Carrington. One day he would destroy Blake Carrington. Blake Carrington made Drake so angry. Unable to bear Blake's arrogance any longer, he flicked back to his South American skirmish and hit the red button. A strategically unimportant shanty town was wiped out in one fabulous conflagration. 'That'll show that blue-rinsed bastard,' he growled.

17

'You took your bloody time,' Edward said as he squinted up through a hole in the tons of rubble and twisted steel at the face of the rescue worker.

'Shut up, you. How's the little girl?'

'She's fine.'

'No I'm not,' Tracey whined, 'I'm in a coma.'

There was an excited murmur behind the rescuer. He turned to face the cameras. 'The girl's in a coma. The teacher's fine.' He turned back to Edward. 'You stay where you are. We're going to bring in some more equipment.'

'What the bloody hell for? We're both okay and we can climb out.'

'The teacher's going delirious. We'll need more equipment,' the rescuer shouted to his team. Behind him, other rescue workers unloaded their space-age gadgets and talked urgently to on-the-spot camera teams. The air was buzzing with the phrases: 'Race against Time', 'Life and Death Drama' and 'Disaster of the Week'.

Edward pulled at Tracey's arm but she fought him off. 'I can't move. I'm still in a coma,' she insisted. Too tired to struggle, Edward let her go and climbed up on his own.

The rescuer looked down in undisguised horror. 'Get back down there,' he snarled. 'Quick. Get the infra-red digger in here!'

A hydraulic scoop with a battery of computer-controlled sensors swung into the hole. With pinpoint accuracy it struck Edward squarely on the forehead and bulldozed him, unconscious, back into the basement. The rescuer sighed. 'Right,' he shouted. 'The teacher's taken quite a bad knock. Bring in the

Resuscitation Unit.' Brightly-overalled, walkie-talkied young men leapt from behind him to perform their melodramatic parts while little birdies went tweet, tweet, tweet round Edward's head.

18

Tom Grimewhistle and Rita Woodley-Mobile stood at the top of the muddy slagheap and peered down through the drizzle. A greasy veil of smoke clung to the rooftops of the blackened factories and tenements below. Tom smiled grimly. 'By 'eck, Rita. Look at that. You can see the whole stinking town from up 'ere,' he snarled, setting his pitted, angular face against the bitter wind. A soft, pre-consumptive cough rattled in his brawny chest. 'All this Nature makes you feel like some passing, minor character in someone else's plot.'

'Oh Tom,' Rita said. 'I can't 'elp feeling there's a poet in you somewhere, despite your rough ways.' She spread a picnic rug out on the damp ground and unpacked their lunch from snap'n'seal boxes. Tom watched Rita's thick, tweed skirt bellow in the chill breeze and caught inviting glimpses of stubble on her chubby calves.

'I'd 'ave my way with you, given half a chance,' he mumbled, pulling down the peak of his cloth cap and diving for her bloomers.

'Tom!' Rita pleaded. 'You know it's impossible. I'm due back at the library in half an hour.'

'Let me keep you a bit longer,' Tom implored, crushing her in his muscular arms. 'I'll pay the fine.'

'No,' said Rita, clamping her knees together. 'There's my husband to think of. And your wife.'

Tom considered the woman he'd left in Reading to take up this new life. 'But they're on 'oliday in Naxos together,' he protested.

'They're bound to suspect.'

'Let them!' Tom picked up a Scotch egg, hurled it out across the moor and held out his arms. 'Let the 'ole 'ypocritical world know. I want to shout it from the roof tops —'

'Tom!'

'"I've 'ad Rita Woodley-Mobile!" — I want to write it in the gents! I want to carve it on the bus-stop! "I've been up Woodley-Mobile!"'

'Tom! You'll do no such thing! —' the sound of a cracking twig caught Rita's ear. 'Tom! Tom! I think someone's watching us.'

'Pull the other one.' Tom strode across the picnic rug and tore open her cardigan with his horny hands.

'Tom!' Rita gasped, kneeing him sharply in the groin. 'You're spilling the Vimto.'

Tom knew he was beaten. Rita was no factory girl. Rita had class. Rita had an authentic and unfastenable fifties bra, and Tom was deeply, hopelessly in love with her. Nursing his injury, he slumped on the edge of the rug and turned on the portable telly. '"Vimto",' he declared angrily, 'is an anagram of "vomit".'

'What a rare, rough diamond of a working class wit you are, Tom,' said Rita. She cracked a hard-boiled egg on her knee and peeled it coquettishly with her teeth, spitting the flakes of shell into the wind. Tom gazed into her tortoiseshell glasses with longing and bit into the lip of his plastic cup. He tossed back the Vimto, swallowed recklessly and turned his eyes to the television to hide his tears.

Rita peeled slices of white bread from a greaseproof paper bag and smeared a pale, lumpy paste on to them with a plastic knife, her little finger standing in proud mockery of Tom's humble origins. Tom kept his eyes to the telly.

On the screen a bubbly newsreader with pink glasses and cuddly features looked earnestly into autocue and ignored the punctuation. 'Welcome back for an update on the story that's really keeping us all glued to the set this Tuesday lunch-time. Yes I'm talking about the school trip that turned into a nightmare. It's been confirmed that only two were caught in yesterday's Baby Burger Bombing. Edward Wilson, the so-called teacher, the demon responsible for the disastrous children's expedition, and tragic Tiny Tracey, the feisty five-year-old who is fighting for her life and winning the hearts of the Environment –'

'Poor little mite,' Rita cooed as Tracey was winched into a helicopter. 'Bit of dripping?'

A saintly, soft-focus shot of Tracey, surrounded by white linen and the latest hospital monitoring equipment, was faded on to the screen. '– Tracey is still in a coma at the Angels of Intensive Private Care Hospital –' said a concerned voice.

'Aw. Look at all them tubes,' said Rita. There was a faint rustle in the undergrowth behind Tom.

'Later we'll be showing exclusive pictures of the dramatic rescue, but first,' the newsreader read cheerily, 'the Leopard and where will he strike next?'

On the screen stood a reporter with bleach-blond hair and a wind-muffler on his microphone. He was standing on a wind-swept moor. 'The Leopard,' he said, 'who seems to favour lonely, open beauty-spots in the North of England, last struck here: one hundred and fifty yards from the road and in broad daylight.'

A hundred and fifty yards to Tom's left, a lone car hurtled past. On screen, a composite impression of the Leopard flashed up – a lean, dark, hairy, lantern-jawed man with a leopard's head for a hat. The computers had spent considerable time composing this image. 'Oooh,' said Rita. 'That's put me right off my bread and dripping.'

Tom turned down the volume and grimaced. 'Rita,' he said, rolling his eyes to show the whites and gurning furiously, 'I am the Leopard. Ha ha! Grrrr!'

'Gerroff, Tom Grimewhistle. It's not funny,' Rita said. He growled and crawled blindly towards her, his arms waving. Rita covered her eyes and turned away. Tom felt a hand grip his shoulder.

'Rita. There's someone's hand —'

'I said, *stop* it!' she shouted. Behind Tom stood a lean, dark, hairy, lantern-jawed man with a leopard's head for a hat. 'Its *THE LEOPARD!!!!!!!!!!!!!!!!!!!!!!!!!!!!!!!!!!!!!!!*' Rita screamed.

The Leopard glowered down at them, cracked his knuckles, curled his lip and growled.

'Rita,' Tom said, nodding towards the lay-by. 'Get up slowly and walk towards the car.' Rita hesitated. 'Do it!' Tom barked. 'Forget the picnic. Go!' The Leopard twisted Tom's head into an anatomically impossible position. Tom smiled with all the sincerity he could muster. 'Now then, Mr Leopard. You've got it all wrong, you see. It's not our lifestyle. We bought the nineteen fifties Northern kitchen sink drama way of life, not yer early seventies psycho nonsense. So, er, if you wouldn't mind —' His voice trailed off.

In the distance, Rita's attempt to start the nineteen fifties replica Ford Popular was futile. The starter motor was especially programmed to encourage illicit, grimy sex in the motoring tradition of the early postwar years.

Lunk tossed his first victim of the day aside and sprinted to the lay-by. He tore off the door of the car and, with the same dexterity he'd applied to Tom Grimewhistle, snapped Rita Woodley-Mobile's neck with a neat and sickening click. He trudged back with Rita's corpse to the abandoned picnic-site and, sharpening his trusty blade, proceeded to watch the end of the newscast.

On Tom and Rita's portable television was a press conference. Strapped to a stretcher outside the Baby Burger Bar, Edward Wilson, already prepared for hospitalization in green, surgical pyjamas, was carried under dazzling halogen lights to face a hostile posse of journalists. 'These were Edward Wilson's first words on emerging,' the newsreader gabbled excitedly.

Lunk's jet-black eyes blazed like anthracite. It was the Different One.

57

'Two Amjap people! They did it! They planted the bomb!' Edward shouted above the baying mob.

'So,' Lunk said half an hour later as he drove a bloodstained fifties replica Ford Popular down the M 1, his voice trembling. 'Edward Wilson. I have found you at last. It's time we joined forces, brother. Together we shall work miracles.'

Tom Grimewhistle was 34. Rita Woodley-Mobile was 32.

19

As the mists of unconsciousness were getting thinner, the first things Edward became aware of were white walls, a splitting headache, deep, rhythmic, painful moans and some equally rhythmic, high whimpers. The headache was definitely his own. The moans and whimpers might have been coming from someone else, though Edward couldn't be sure.

Memory was returning in fragments, indistinguishable from the headache and the moaning. They recalled hours of torment. 'Let me get out! I can get out!' Edward screamed, not aware if this was still a dream, the memory of a dream, the recent past or the present.

Dr Kiley quickly withdrew from the nurse and rolled on to his feet. 'Thank you, nurse. That will be all,' he said, applying a surgical swab and glancing over at the patient.

'I think I'm coming round,' Edward moaned.

Kiley's movements were swift and decisive. 'I'll do the professional diagnosis, if you don't mind,' he whispered angrily. He glanced back at the nurse as she zipped herself back into her skimpy uniform. He placed a stethoscope to the side of Edward's monitor and frowned. He turned up the volume. He frowned again. The nurse came to stand behind him. Kiley took a rubber hammer from his pocket and tapped the top of the cardioencephalogram. 'Aha,' he said as he ran his palm along the surface of the screen, rapping the back of his hand with his knuckles. He frowned again. The nurse held her breath. 'Stand by, nurse. He's coming round. I'm adjusting his vertical hold.'

The nurse dashed to the chart at the end of Edward's bed

and scribbled an entry. Kiley shot her a stern look which broke into a heartbreakingly reassuring smile. The effect was devastating. The nurse gazed back and melted. She dashed into his arms. Kiley smoothed her blonde hair tenderly and kissed her deeply, passionately. 'He's going to be all right. It's up to him, of course, but he may just pull through,' Kiley murmured as he nuzzled her ear. Those smooth, firm, deft, skilful, reassuring hands of his, those perfectly manicured doctor's hands, slid comfortingly up the back of her naked thighs and into her knickers. The chart fell to the floor.

'Excuse me,' said Edward, blinking at them. 'I'm not unconscious any more, you know.'

Kiley disengaged himself with clinical precision. The nurse swayed in a state of bewildered sexual hiatus. 'Better get his agent in,' Kiley said. The nurse's eyes swam dreamily towards his. 'Well, don't just stand there, nurse! Jump to it!' he barked. Her face crumpled into a crimson mess. Hiding her shame in her hands, she stumbled out into the corridor.

Edward grimaced. 'Doctor, I seem to have a terrible headache and I can't remember why.'

'I've already told you,' Kiley snapped. '*I'm* the doctor. When you've got a headache, you will please allow me the discretion to diagnose it.'

'Sorry. Forgot. Must be suffering from amnesia.'

'Oh. So you *are* a doctor, are you?'

'Am I?'

'No. You're a patient. Kindly remember that.'

'So, what's my condition, doctor?'

Kiley ripped a printout from a box by Edward's head and shook his head. He tapped a few buttons, sniffed and looked grave. 'Tracey Wex's parents are suing you.'

'Right. That's decided, I'm giving up teaching.'

Suddenly the door was kicked open. A young man, an Italian suit, a pair of mauve glasses, a floral tie and a Filofax burst into the room in loose formation. The young man's right arm shook a sheaf of papers at the bed. 'You irresponsible swine! Filth! You callous monster!' he screamed.

Kiley glowered at the nurse in the doorway. 'Nurse, I thought you might at least be able to manage *one* simple request!' he said. 'Get the press out of here and find Mr Wilson's agent.' Tears welled up in her powder-blue eyes.

'But doctor,' she pointed to the young man who was glancing at Edward's chart, 'that *is* his agent.'

The agent glared up from the chart, lowered his face right into Edward's and shouted: 'Monster! Filth! Child-molester! Perv!'

Kiley swept over to the nurse. His eyes burned into hers. 'I've been such a terrible fool,' he said. 'Can you ever forgive me? I never want to lose you, Jane.' He took her in his arms. The nurse swooned as their lips touched and she knew she would never be unhappy again. Her name wasn't Jane, but what the hell.

The young man stubbed a thumb at the couple as they shuffled out of the room and winked. 'Bloody lifestylists. Give me the real thing any day. Gordon Blank's the name. Blank by name, blank by nature. I'm going to represent you as your sole — and when I say sole, I mean multiple — personal P R consultant.' He shook Edward's hand and smiled. 'Excited? You betcha! We're gonna have some funeroony together.' Edward closed his eyes and opened them, but the vision of bad high-street fashion was still there.

'I don't need you. I need, if anything, a real doctor.' Gordon shook his head.

'Now that's just where you're wrong.' He squared his padded shoulders and drew a deep breath. 'You see, Edward — that little audiovisual demonstration I just gave (with no meter running, I might add) is the kind of the thing the *papers* are saying about you. They've got this idea you should never have taken the children to the Baby Burger Bar.' He paused and smiled. 'Now this is BIG.'

'Look. Two AmJap people blew up that building. They're to blame. Not me.'

'Er, well, er, good point. Good point. We can use that. Somewhere. Now, look. I've been in PR a long time —'

'Help!' Edward wailed, passing out under the strain. 'Help me . . .'

'Help? Help you?' Gordon stammered. 'Right. You need me. I smell big moolah here. For both of us, of course,' he added, grinning. He sat down on the bed and flicked through his Filofax. 'How would it be if I called you Eddie?'

'Grisly,' Edward moaned from the depths.

'That's what I thought.'

Half an hour later, when Edward opened his eyes, Gordon was still there and still talking. '—and another thing. Have you seen the papers? Here.' He handed Edward a selection of front pages, ranging from: TWISTED TEACHER FROM HELL to TINY TRACEY IN NIGHTMARE COMA — TEACHER TO BLAME.

'She's not in a coma,' Edward said hoarsely. 'She's faking.' Gordon nodded.

'Sure. Now. The press position on you is what we in the biz call justifiable anger. But how about if you'd been more seriously injured? We could get you as much sympathy as the Wex kid. Bingo. Exclusives all round, everyone happy. No more blame.' He made a circle with his thumb and forefinger and winked.

'But I'm *not* seriously injured, am I?'

Gordon checked a printout. 'No. Exactly. You've grasped the nettle. Now shut your eyes. You won't feel a thing.' He wrenched a length of heavy steel tubing from Edward's bed and began slapping it in his palm. Edward pointed a quivering finger.

'What are you going to do with that?'

'I just explained all that. I'm going to hit you with it. To adapt a well known adage, you need me *and* a hole in the head.' He flashed a smile. 'Trust me.'

In another part of the hospital a grey-haired doctor gently held the tiny, nailvarnished hand of the Environment's most celebrated feisty little five-year-old girl. Above her head, both brain and heart scanners registered a deep and probably irreversible coma. The doctor's adam's apple bobbed as he whispered in her ear. 'Tracey, this is your own very special doctor. Please. We all love you. If you can hear me, please, please, please, please open your eyes.' Tracey's lids remained closed. 'Gee, what a great kid you are,' he sighed, wiping away a tear. 'I just want you to know that this hospital is going to do everything in its power to make you all better, because we want —'

Suddenly the door to the room swung open and Edward slithered over the shiny floor in his hospital bed-socks and crashed into the bed.

'What's going on?' the doctor protested. 'This is *my* session. I'm hoping against hope for a miracle here and it's *my* turn!'

'If you don't push off,' Edward shoved his bandaged head close to the doctor's face, 'I'm going to ram that stethoscope so far down your throat that one fart will deafen you for life.'

'Alright, alright. I'll come back later.' He retreated through the door. Edward hitched himself on to the bed, checked the scanners and, taking Tracey by the neck, shook her violently.

Tracey opened her eyes and eased his hands from her neck. She smiled languorously. 'Oh, hallo, Edward. I was wondering when you'd come and see me,' she said.

'Listen, I haven't got much time. I've just escaped from my agent. You've got to help me.'

'Shshs . . .' She pressed a ringed forefinger to his lips to silence him. 'It's so lovely to talk to you. Being in a coma's really boring. Entertain me. Amuse me.' She folded her arms and simpered. Edward stifled a sob.

'Please. Look. No more coma, okay? You've had your bit of fun, but let's stop before it ends in tears.' Tears of his own were beginning to brim in his eyes.

'No,' said Tracey. 'My fun's only just started. I'm going to have pop stars in here, Mum and Dad are going to make a fortune and I'm going to be as famous as Tabafa Minx. Famouser!' She clapped her hands together and squeezed them.

'When my agent catches up with me he's going to smash my skull in because people believe you. You've got to stop faking this coma . . .' Edward let the sob go. Tracey patted a spot on the bed.

'I hate seeing grown-ups cry. Come and sit here.' Edward edged up, looking anxiously back at the door. The scanners began to bleep faster and louder. 'Get up, you stupid idiot! Mind Bertie.' The screens above her head no longer indicated a coma, had gone past registering a healthy child and now depicted a sprinter at full stretch. She pushed Edward back and smoothed the sheets. The representation of deep coma returned to the monitors.

Edward's eyes narrowed. He plucked at the wires running from the array of monitors and followed them under the sheets. Tracey tried to hold them down, but he burrowed for all he was worth. Adult strength won over at last. There in the bed, wrapped in a tiny space blanket, at the centre of a network of wires and electrodes, was a hibernating horseshoe bat. Edward squeezed it gently. The monitors spiralled, the blips pinged louder. 'This, I take it,' he said. 'is Bertie?'

Tracey's nose crinkled. 'Yes. It's brilliant. His heart beats ten times a minute and his brain activity's virtually non-existent. It's the deepest coma the doctor's ever seen.'

'Well, I'm sorry, Tracey, but your dreams of superstardom are over.' Edward grasped Bertie tighter and yelled into his ear. 'Wake up Bertie! It's springtime!' Tracey leapt forward.

'I'll bloody kill you,' she squealed, pulling her end of Bertie with all her might.

The door flew open and through it stormed five burly porters, led by Gordon Blank. Edward dropped Bertie and dived for the window. Gordon tackled him to the ground. Ignoring the struggle, Tracey rearranged her bed and shut her eyes tight. Bertie returned to hibernation and the machines resumed their slow blipping as Edward's shoulders were secured by the knees of two large men. He twisted under their grip. 'Gordon. There's a bat in that bed,' he said.

'Sure, Eddie,' said Gordon, swinging a claw-hammer. 'Sure. But the public regard her as a five-year-old girl. Now, hold him down, lads.' He wagged an admonishing finger. 'Remember: I'm your personal representative and I know what I'm doing.'

'You're fired! You're fired!' Edward screamed.

'Hold him tight,' said Gordon licking his lips and taking a bead on Edward's bandaged cranium 'because this bit's bloody dangerous.'

There was a loud crack. Edward slipped over the edge and into blackness. 'Okay,' said Gordon. 'Alert the operating theatre. We need an E C G, whole blood, plasma ... Oh, and set up a press room.' He turned smartly on his heel and marched out, singing a line from his favourite song. 'We're in the money ...'

20

Dr Kiley glanced up from the table and flicked a scalpel into a kidney dish with a clattering flourish. 'Okay, nurse, I've done all the cool, macho cutting and drilling bits. Now it's your turn to do all the silly, girly bits like sewing.' The nurse radiated gratitude.

'Will Mr Wilson ever recover his eyesight?' she asked. Kiley considered the point for a fraction of a second.

'How should I know? We're insured, aren't we?'

Suddenly one of the other nurses gasped in horror. 'Oh, no! Dr Kiley! It's half past eight! Your favourite programme's just starting on Channel Twenty-Six!' This was just the kind of emergency he had trained for. He acted. Fast.

'I know,' he grinned. 'Reconnect cardioencephalogram to Channel Twenty-Six.' The team tore at the sensors attached to Edward's head and fiddled with the switches on the back of the machine. The nurse wiped another bead of perspiration from Kiley's forehead. He looked at her sharply.

'Doctor, what is it?'

'Get me a six-pack. And some cheese dip would be nice.'

'Yes, Dr Kiley.' She gazed adoringly into his smooth, handsome face.

'Nurse. Are you going to get it or stand around agreeing with me?'

'Oh, I . . .'

'Run along, you silly little thing,' he chuckled, patting her bottom. She blushed and tripped lightly from the room, her heart singing.

The rest of the team assembled around the cardioencephalogram. It was showing the popular and absolutely unmissable weekly viewing for all medics, the hospital sitcom 'I'm Losing My Patients!', and joined in with the canned laughter.

'Oh oh urrr ... nnnnn ... I know I'm not a doctor, but I think I'm coming round,' Edward moaned on the operating table, straining to get up. The team hooted at each terrible joke on the screen. One of the instruments fell off the table. Kiley looked back.

'Shshsh!'

Edward swivelled his eyes and blinked rapidly. 'I can't see!' he wailed.

'Shut up, Mr Wilson. You're *supposed* to be under anaesthetic,' Kiley commanded. Edward directed his eyes around the room.

'Someone turn the lights on,' he groaned.

'Look, Wilson,' Kiley shouted, 'they *are* on. You're blind. Now just bloody shut up.'

'Blind? What, permanently?' Kiley dragged his attention from the screen.

'How the hell do I know? We'll try shock treatment sometime. That'll be jolly. Look. Can we have this conversation later? This is a good bit.' He turned back just in time to watch the sitcom operating theatre explode.

'BLIND!!??'

'SHUT UP!' everyone shouted.

Edward struggled from under the bedsheet and flopped on to the lino, sending kidney dishes and surgical instruments spinning across the theatre. Trailing plastic tubes, wires and bandages, he fumbled away from the operating table, his arms outstretched. 'Where's the door?' he asked.

'Over there!' someone laughed.

Edward swung round to where he imagined the medical team were sitting. 'Don't you people realize these bombs are coming from the AmJap Corporation? They're up to something, you know,' he said to a line of washbasins. Behind him, the laughter continued to rise and fall. He felt his way along the wall until part of it swung open. Gingerly, he padded into the corridor.

In the operating theatre next door, one of the few real doctors still practising in the Environment was up to her elbows in someone's chest. With a loud squelching she pulled out the heart and held it steaming in her hands. 'Is the transplant bag ready?' The male nurse assisting her had stuffed padding into one of his shoulders and drawn stitches across his forehead with a biro. He rolled his tongue across his lips and crossed his eyes.

'Ye-es, doctorr. Eet ees time to geev yorr creeeation . . . life! ha ha aha . . .'

She slopped the heart into the bag and snapped it shut. 'Will you please stop fartarsing around? Dr Blatt has got an hour to get this heart to the recipient in Milton Keynes.' She turned to the nurse. He was now sporting a leather flying hat and a handlebar moustache, both secured with elastic. 'Please try to take this seriously . . .' she sighed.

'Okay, chaps. Scramble. Chocks away.' He snatched the bag in his teeth and zoomed out into the corridor, holding his arms outstretched and making dagadagadagadaga noises. The surgeon slumped over the inert body on the table and abandoned herself to tears.

The nurse crashed almost immediately into a man in green, surgical pyjamas. 'Listen! All of you,' the man said. 'There is an AmJap conspiracy to destroy the Environment and I'm completely blind!'

The heart-bag slid under a nearby wheelchair as they fell wrestling to the floor. The nurse disentangled himself, tore off his costume and slapped on a Groucho Marx moustache with attached nose and glasses. 'Ah, you don't fool me so easy, Dr Blatt,' he said in pure Bronx, tapping the ash from an imaginary cigar and reaching over for the heart. 'Here you are.' He thrust it on to Edward's chest. Edward held it limply.

'What is it?'

'My heart. Take it back to San Francisco via Milton Keynes and don't spare the horses.' He beckoned the wheelchair over. 'Escort Dr Blatt to the car. The plane's waiting on the runway.'

'Certainly,' said the wheelchair.

'I've gone mad!' Edward screamed as the wheelchair scooped him up and whizzed him off down the corridor.

'Come with me, Dr Blatt,' it said.

'I'm not Dr Blatt. I'm Edward Wilson.'

The wheelchair accelerated to breakneck pace. 'Gawd. Like a madhouse in here today,' it said. They whirred through reception and out into the car-park. The wheelchair bundled him into the back seat of a car, slammed the door and bashed the roof with one of its metal arms. 'Go to the airport and step on it,' it said. The car smashed itself into gear and burned rubber.

21

Archie McNee squinted through the thick, blue haze of the conference room and watched as another of his feature writers slid from his perch and slumped with an explosive fart on to the beer-stained carpet. McNee surveyed the rest of his staff as they lurched around the room, whisky bottles in hand, cannoning into the furniture and shouting boisterous obscenities.

'You there,' he shouted to the least inebriated-looking journalist. 'Get Nik back on his feet.' The man swayed over, clawed at the collar of his inert colleague and pitched over on top of him. They lay on the carpet, murmuring endearments to a bottle of vodka clutched between their four hands. The news team began to sing a medley of anatomical songs. McNee climbed on to his desk and turned up the volume on his megaphone. 'This is supposed to be an editorial meeting. Please try and behave like top journalists.'

The men suppressed giggles, straightened their ties and turned unsteadily to listen to their boss. McNee sat down on the edge of his desk and scanned a single sheet of paper which the computer had just fed to him. 'Right. Main stories. The Leopard is on the move. Fresh killings in Accrington. Massive increase in the number of bombings everywhere. Tuck that one in on page eight somewhere. Latest opinion poll shows that –'

The door was flung open and Tabafa Minx jogged in, naked but for a pair of little running weights in her hands, a pink sweatband, a silver lurex G-string and some blue, spray-on nipple glitter. She placed her ample, pink bottom on McNee's desk and smouldered at him. Before a word could leave her fabulous, pouting lips, George Minx, sweating heavily into his sheepskin coat and trilby, waddled through the open door, advanced on the desk and drew his portly body to its full height.

'Awright, Tab. I'll deal wiv this. McNee!' Mr Minx roared.

McNee reddened. 'Mr Minx! I cannot have pin-ups barging in here with their dads and disrupting very serious and important discussions.' His staff gave drunken murmurs.

'Mr McNee. As Tabafa Minx's sole father, agent and manager –' Tabafa rolled her gorgeous, turquoise eyes skywards.

'Get on wiv it, Dad.'

'Awright, princess,' George patted her silken shoulder. 'No. Mr McNee. As Tabafa Minx's sole father, agent and personal manager, I am alarmed to note that my daughter, client and chief asset (i.e. Tabafa Minx, Star of Page and Screen) has not been seen, witnessed or oggled at in any media or medium in the last two days.'

'Yeah,' Tabafa added with an aggrieved pout.

McNee's grey eyes became slits. 'I'm sorry, but the Mainframe Computer is in constant touch with public opinion and in the latest poll ninety-four per cent, when asked, said that you was yesterday's pin-up. You're finished.'

Mr Minx shrank visibly. He fumbled for his hip flask, took a long swig and shook. 'But she's my only daughter,' he croaked, shooting Tabafa a savage glance. 'I knew we should have had more!' Tabafa pulled off her sweatband and shook out her glossy, red mane.

'So, that's it, then, is it?'

A snigger circulated through the hacks. McNee shook his head. 'Oh, no. You're still newsworthy. You've got about three weeks of "Cruel Media World Jilts Totty Tab" and your sad decline into alcoholism.'

George wiped his lips with the back of his hand and cast a worried look over his daughter. 'What am I going to tell your Mum?' he said. Tabafa shrugged her shoulders and tickled him under the chin.

'Cheer up. We done alright. We invested, didn't we?'

'Tabafa,' Mr Minx said in his deepest, father-knows-best voice. 'Part and parcel of any investment is an element of risk . . .'

'Yeah?'

'And none of my horses came in.'

'You gambled my money away on the gee-gees!'

'*Our* money, princess. *Our* money,' said George, backing away.

'Right. We'll really have to really pull out the stops now. And from now on,' she shot him her most gorgeous Venomous Vixen ever. '*I'm* looking after the money.'

'Would you kindly conduct your industrial dispute outside my office? We're trying to hold a meeting,' McNee blurted, resorting once more to the megaphone. George took the hint full in the left ear and staggered off to the lift.

'I'm not finished yet, Mr McNee!' said Tabafa, thrusting out her chest and causing three journalists to faint. 'Wherever the big news is, that's where you'll find me. I'm gonna stay Number One.' She jogged out of the room. The men dissolved into hysterical laughter.

The laughter stopped dead as, without warning, the Mainframe burst into life. McNee ripped the paper from its printout. 'Stack me!' he exclaimed. The men looked expectantly to their editor. McNee read from the sheet. '"Edward Wilson, Baby Burger Bar Teacher in Milton Keynes Heart Swap Mercy Flight"! It's a big story.' The hacks jumped up on to their desks and performed a war dance. McNee eyed them proudly. 'Right, lads. Get yer drinking gear on. We're off to Milton Keynes.' He toppled and fell under the stampede.

22

Safe within the glass walls of the AmJap Environment headquarters building, high up on the five-hundredth floor, Colonel Brad Matterhorn lay on his platinum cot, a high-tension electric cable strapped tightly to his left arm. A low, electrical hum pulsed through him. His body twitched and flexed. AmJap technical wizardry whirred and bleeped on the walls. Across the floor, banks of screens were monitoring the destruction of prime Environment real estate. He sat bolt upright, his head jerking from side to side in violent spasms. 'Twang!' He barked. Twang swivelled sharply from his desk.

'Yes, Colonel Matterhorn, sir?'

Brad stared wildly. 'What's happening?' Twang punched a button and read from one of the screens at his console.

'We-ell sur. We done gone barmed another tharty-three build'n's 'fore twe-elve hundred hours, all leave is cancelled and we got the dee-struction agents working round the clock.' Twang swallowed nervously. 'Er. One or two o' the'agents're showing' sahns o' fatigue, sur.'

Brad's twitching face turned thunderous. 'So? Treble the rate. I need this dump colonized in under three weeks.' Twang threw him a salute and a nervous glance.

'Sur. CL 'n' Bushido, the Baby Burger Bar operatives're comin' up to see you, sur.' Brad's eyes gleamed.

'Good. Those two screwed up. You know what Rule Number One in this ball game is, Twang?' Twang shook his head. 'Don't screw up.' Brad's body thrashed in the cot like a landed fish. Twang dashed over.

'Shall I unplug you now, sur?'

'Go ahead.' Twang snapped off a switch in the wall. The

electrical hum stopped. Brad uncoiled, ripped the cable off his arm and stretched, massaging his neck. 'Phew. I love electricity. All my life I've loved its power; it's so pure, so efficient, so . . .' He squinted at the ceiling. '. . . so sexy.'

'Sexy, sur?'

'Sure. You know. As it courses through your body you get a feeling of . . . of . . .' Again he searched the air.

'Pain, sur?'

'Pain. Sweet, cleansing pain. It's honest. Here. Try some.' He offered Twang the cable.

'Thank you, sur, but Ah just took lunch.'

'You don't know what you're missing.' Brad leapt from the cot. 'It kinda makes you feel tingly all over,' he said. His crew-cut was topped with a blue halo, his eyes burning like ultraviolet lasers. 'It's what gives me a healthy glow.'

'Suits you, sur.' Brad gave him a folksy smile.

'Thank you, Twang. I wanna shake your hand,' said Brad. Twang left the ground as several thousand volts shot into his body. 'Ha ha! Better than a joy buzzer!'

The lift door slid open. Bushido and CL flew in, shot to attention and snapped a salute. Brad appraised them, stepped over Twang and walked slowly towards them. He held his face six inches from Bushido's forehead, then six inches from CL's chin. He stepped back. 'Now, my top destruction agents, how was the bombing of the Baby Burger Bar?'

CL swallowed hard, looked straight ahead and kept her eyes unfocused. 'Just routine, sir.'

'Sure?'

'Sure, sir,' Bushido nodded.

'Aha. Okay. Well, let's take a look, shall we?' He snapped his fingers at Twang who hauled himself up and punched a button on his desk. On the main wallscreen appeared the rescue pictures from the night before. A large cursor arrow highlighted Edward. 'Boy, you two really screwed up,' Brad drawled.

'I'm not at liberty to disclose the nature and details of any operation that may or may not have occurred, sir,' said CL.

'What is this bullshit?'

'If such a hypothetical mission were to have taken place, sir, then its result, if it had occurred, would be nonexistent, sir.' Bushido hung his head.

'So. We have failed.' CL glared at him.

'I must request that my colleague's statement be deleted from the record, sir.'

'Our honour is besmirched!' Bushido spluttered.

'The AmJap Corporation is not concerned with personal vanity,' Brad erupted, punching a bright blue finger into each of their stomachs and making them leap. 'It has a higher cause. Now get back in the field, find this gook Wilson and await further orders.'

They snapped a salute and marched from the room.

23

The old Dakota levelled off. Taggart, the weatherbeaten pilot, slid back in his Jason Recliner and swapped a toothsome smile with Patton, a particularly ugly bulldog with a leather patch over one eye. Taggart was a tough, ruggedly handsome, gung-ho ex fighter pilot from the New Territories.

He cocked his head to the back of the plane and checked the cargo area. His passenger was still stumbling up and down the fuselage and flaying the air with his hands. 'Jeez, Patton, that Dr Blatt's a right windy ratbag,' he said. 'You okay in the back of the plane?'

Edward turned in the direction of the voice. 'Oh. Thank you. I'm in the back of a *plane*, am I? I'm blind, you know. What the hell's going on?'

'Cripes, you poms have got a funny sense of humour,' Taggart laughed. He scanned the dials and keyed his mike. 'Er . . . Hallo tower, this is Oscar Vector Tango twenty degrees bearing two point blah de blah de blah. I'll do the drop an' if the law isn't up my arse I'll hang a Uie, whatever that means, over and out.' He threw Patton the crust of a Vegemite sandwich, released the controls and stood up. 'You look as lonely as a bastard on Father's Day back there,' he shouted.

Edward heard the clump of boots and felt a hard muscular hand grasp his own.

'Hi. Don't worry. I'm an Australian. I'm flying this crate. This is General Patton.' Edward recoiled from the dank, doggy breath. 'How's the heart?' Taggart gesticulated towards the transplant bag. Edward patted his own chest.

'Recovering.'

'Not yours, y'ol' bastard. That one. Been on many mercy

76

missions before?' Edward shook his head. Taggart squatted down next to him and took out some rolling 'baccy. 'Me neither. Done everything else, though. Whisky runs, drugs, rifles, them little bakelite coasters that go under sofa legs. Did that for about eight years.'

Taggart leant forward and lowered his voice. 'Actually, to tell you the truth, I've only been doing this for a couple of weeks. I absolutely love it, though. I can't help feeling it's really *me*, if you know what I mean.' He stuck the badly-rolled cigarette in his mouth and stood up. 'We'll be over the hospital in about ten minutes. I'll tell you when to jump.'

'Jump?'

'Well, you can't *walk* down, can you?' Taggart scooped up a parachute pack and pulled Edward's arms and legs through the straps. ''S easy. Jus' count to ten and pull the ripcord,' he said, tightening the buckles. 'At least, I think that's what you do.'

Edward struggled to free himself. 'Shouldn't you be at the controls?' he suggested.

'No prob, Kidderooni. Take over, Patton!' Patton barked and scampered off towards the flight cabin, stopping on the way to sniff the heart-bag and cock his leg. 'Now we're going to see some flying,' said Taggart. '*He* loves it. Scares the crap out of me.' He wrenched open a small door. 'That's why I let him do it. I'm in the dunny if anyone wants me.' He swung himself in and slammed the door.

Edward felt himself sliding along the floor towards the cockpit. The engines were screaming louder and louder. He clawed his way up the almost vertical slope and hammered the walls with his fists. 'Taggart! Taggart!' he bellowed. His fingers found a metal catch on the wall. 'If you don't come out I'm going to break the door down and drag you out!' He tugged at the catch with all his might. The main cargo door burst open with an explosion of slipstream. Edward shot screaming into a whirlwind of cold air.

'Phew! Wouldn't go in there for a minute,' said Taggart, backing out of the toilet door and beating the air with his hand. He looked down at the open door. 'Streuth. Little sookie's gone walkabout. Could at least have shut the door.' Fighting the fierce gale in the fuselage, he heaved the hatch shut, shouldered the heart-bag and let himself tumble back into the cockpit. The altimeter was spinning anticlockwise. Through the windscreen and dead ahead, the Home Counties were getting closer. He hauled on the stick. After a stomach-churning lurch, Hertfordshire levelled off and fell away again. 'Better get this heart to Milton Keynes, I suppose,' Taggart shrugged. 'Stick a cassette in, ol' buddy.' Patton nudged a tape in with his nose and Rolf Harris's Greatest Hit filled the cockpit. 'Ripper!' said Taggart.

24

Norbert Seriously, in a tie-dye cheesecloth shirt, faded flared jeans, open-toed sandals, grey nylon socks and a bandanna round his frizzy ginger wig, stood picking his nose on the muddy verge of the slip-road to Junction 12 of the M1 and watched a car approaching. He held out his thumb for the eight-hundredth-and-forty-second time and shouted. 'Bum me a ride, baby!' The car sprayed him with mud and accelerated past. He threw an inverted peace sign after it. 'Square!' He picked up a thick instruction manual entitled *Hippy Lifestyle* and leafed through it. He hadn't got far into the first paragraph when he was distracted by the sound of an aeroengine. He scanned the sky.

The plane was a Dakota. Norbert had made quite a few of them in his Airfix days, though he'd never quite got round to putting the transfers on. He wished he was in that groovy aeroplane. He hooked his thumb at it and watched to see if it would slow down. He saw the silhouette of a tiny, weeny little man jump out. 'Blimey,' he said, 'I'm on a trip!' He reflected for a moment. His landlady, Mrs Wigge, had refused to pack any drugs. 'Oh, *man*! It must be real. That's unreal, man. What a bummer.'

He was just flicking through the index of the manual, when Edward smashed him into the ground and enveloped him in a purple parachute.

Edward rolled around under the parachute and kissed the soggy grass. Norbert scrambled out. Inside, Edward was doing a dance and shouting with joy. 'My eyes! I can see a purple mist!' he exclaimed.

'So what?' said Norbert. 'That's because you've got a bloom-in' parachute over your head.'

'Can you help me get out then, please?'

Norbert tried but the silk twisted tighter as Edward kicked and rolled around inside. 'Your karma's all mucked up in there,' he said. 'You should get more laid back. Your problem is you don't know where you're at. I was just the same until I hit the road.'

'I'm glad I hit the grass, actually.'

'Wow! Grass? Fantastic! I've been standing here since yesterday, you know. I'm busting for a joint. How did you get a lift off that plane? I can't even get a little *car* to stop for me.' Edward was struggling hard. Norbert extended a hand. 'By the way. Why don't you take that parachute off?' Edward tore a hole in his cocoon. His bandages had slipped and were hanging over his face.

'I can see lights! Bright lights!' Edward said, ripping the bandages away and squinting at the horizon. Norbert gaped at the pyjamas and held out his arms.

'Hey. That's far out! Sometimes *I* see things, you know. Really freaky.' He held up his lunch box. 'Agh! My sandwiches are turning into a freaky psychedelic train-set!' Edward stared in wonder.

'I'm not blind!' he yelled.

'You can see it as well? Triffic, man! We're sharing the trip.' Norbert dropped his lunch box and rifled through the pages of his manual. 'I'd better look that one up.'

Edward focused on Norbert. 'What have you come as?' he asked. Norbert flicked back a lock of ginger wig.

'I'm hitchhiking for Free Love and not going to Vietnam because it's full of communists and freaking out. Watch this.' He clutched his temples and writhed on the ground. 'Aaaaaahhh! Where's my head gone?' Edward kicked him in the ribs.

'Which way's London? I've got to tell the world about these AmJap people.'

'Wow. You're really far out. You a hospital doctor? I love your jimjams. Do you think *I* could be a hospital doctor?'

Edward's attention was caught by a line of speeding cars roaring northwards, their headlights blazing and styrofoam cups flying from the windows. He waved his arms and ran down the embankment.

25

Hearing the Wilson Heart-Swap Mercy Dash story on the car radio, Lunk hurriedly abandoned the fifties replica Ford Popular on the wrong side of the M1 and made his way cross-country to the nearest populated area. He found himself watching a typical Environment family through the double-glazing of their ground-floor living room.

26

The last car in the convoy screeched to a halt and the driver's window buzzed down. Norbert skidded down the muddy slope, jostled himself in behind Edward and presented his thumb. 'Bum me a ride, baby!' he said. A synthesized voice issued from the dashboard in front of the empty driver's seat. 'Hallo, old chap. Which way you going?'

'London,' said Edward.

'Oh dear. You're on the wrong side of the road, I'm afraid. I'm taking my passenger to Milton Keynes.' The window buzzed back up.

'Cuh. *I* could've told you that,' said Norbert.

Edward snatched at the door handle. 'Wait! That'll do.'

'Yeah. Right on, let's take this mood buggy to Crystal Nowhere'sville.'

The window buzzed back down again. 'I'll take you, but not that ghastly hippy,' said the driver. Pushing Norbert aside, Edward jumped into the back seat. The car pulled away sharply and ran over Norbert's foot. Norbert hopped into the road.

'Wow, cars can be really unfeeling, man!' he shouted.

Sprawled out asleep next to Edward was a fat, middle-aged man with a scarlet nose. The automatic driver cleared its electronic throat. 'Ahem. You a doctor, then?'

'No, I'm –'

'Oh dear. Riff-raff. Only pick up professionals as a rule.'

From somewhere else on the dashboard the voice of the onboard radar cut into the conversation. 'Warning, warning. Obstruction ahead.' The car throttled back. Edward nodded to the sleeping man. 'What's *he* do?'

'Journalist. Big story in Milton Keynes.'

'Warning. Obstruction ahead,' the radar bleated again.

The car slowed to cruising speed just as another car screamed past and cut in front of them, forcing the automatic driver to swerve violently. 'Gad! Look at that idiot. Italian cars have motorway madness. Don't worry about me, by the way. I'm fail-safe.'

'Warning. Obstruction three hundred metres ahead. Switching to Safety –'

Edward felt a terrible jolt and shot head over heels into the front seat. The next few seconds were filled with more screeching, tearing, crashing, roaring, lurching, tumbling, rolling and twisting than Edward could possibly make sense of.

27

The car had come to an abrupt halt. Tangled into the bonnet was the rear of the Italian car that had just overtaken them. The Italian car seemed to be tangled up with a German one in front of that. In front of that was a confused heap of other write-offs, their radiators hissing steam, their automatic fire extinguishers spewing foam across the road. Somewhere in the middle of the heap was a fifties replica Ford Popular.

'Would you mind extinguishing all cigarettes? Just pull down the oxygen masks and breath normally,' the driver said dryly as a hundred and twenty gallons of flame-retardant foam gushed into the interior.

The journalist woke with a start. 'We here already, driver?'

'Multiple pile-up, old boy.'

The journalist nodded calmly. 'Who the hell are you?' he said, noticing Edward crouched under the dashboard. Edward tried but failed to form a single word. 'Shame,' said the man, heaving a fat shoulder against the door. 'Only got this car last week.' The door swung open and fell off.

Edward struggled out on to the road. Swaying unsteadily in the ankle-deep foam, the journalist whistled his appreciation. The entire Fleet Street convoy was enmeshed in an automotive orgy. Drink-sodden journalists were wriggling out of the mess like maggots from a huge carcass. Those with cameras were taking shots of the ones still trapped in the mangled cars.

A well-known body appeared suddenly from one of the cars and began hopping around the heap. 'Help! Help! I've lost all my clothes, I've lost all my clothes!' she squealed, stopping occasionally for an alluring pose.

'Don't miss a trick, do she? That girl's a real pro.' said the journalist, shaking his head.

The cameramen abandoned DEATH PILE-UP TRAGEDY OF THE WEEK to shout instructions for GORGEOUS TAB GIVES RELIEF TO DYING JOURNALISTS. 'Drape yourself over the car, Tab. That's it. Look sexy. Sexy but disturbed. Lovely.' Motor-drives whirred and video cameras hummed.

'Oi! What about the human angle? I'm injured!' wailed one of the journalists still wedged under the cars. Tabafa raced over.

'What about if I rescue him? How's that? What's yer name, darlin'?' she asked.

'Garf,' he croaked.

'Give us a smile, Garf. You're gonna be famous!' She tugged at Garth's fractured arm and pushed out her chest. Garth screamed. The motor-drives went crazy.

'Great, Tab. Lovely!' someone said. 'Gordon Bennett. 'Course – needs a doctor, dunnit? Oi, you! Doctor!' He beckoned to Edward. Edward edged away.

'I'm not a doctor,' he pleaded. Strong hands propelled him forward.

'So what? You *look* like one. You mop the nice doctor-man's brow, Tabby, while he tries to pull Garf out from under his car.' A barrage of instructions nudged and prodded the story into shape. The cameras went into turbodrive as Edward tugged lamely at Garth's trousers. Tabafa mopped his brow as Garth screamed in agony.

'Shuddup, Garf. We'll do the soundtrack later. Lovely. Come on, Tab. Nice kiss for the doctor . . .'

Tabafa wrapped her arms around Edward's neck and placed her marshmallow lips to his cheek. Pulling away sharply, she eyed him with suspicion. ''Ere. Don't I know you?' she said. Edward dropped Garth's leg.

'Hyde Park. Three days ago.'

Grinning broadly at the cameras, Tabafa wreathed her arms round his waist and squeezed him tightly. ''Ere. You done awright. Twice on telly with me in three days. People might start linking' our names if you're lucky.'

Edward sank into her bosom and thought. 'Oh, yes. They're bound to. I'm Edward Wilson, the Pedagogue of Doom, and I've got something very important to announce to the press, you know. Big News,' he said.

'Blimey. You're just the bloke I've bin lookin' for.'

''Ere. It's Wilson. The big story!' one of the journalists shouted. Tabafa hugged Edward and licked his neck.

'We're 'aving an affair! That's official!' she announced.

Banks of microphones were thrust into their faces. Edward pulled a microphone to his mouth. 'Listen. When I arrived in the Baby Burger Bar with the children, there were two –'

'Mr Wilson. How long have you been having your torrid affair with Miss Minx?'

'Listen to me. I'm trying to tell you about –'

'We were childhood sweethearts, and although I became famous, Edward continued to admire me from afar. Sadly we grew apart. But now he's famous, naturally we're together again and –'

Edward raised his hand for silence. 'Listen. All of you. I'd like to make a very important statement to you . . .'

28

They were slumped on the sofa in front of a TV wallscreen.
A child was jumping up and down next to its mother. 'I want
one! I want one!' it yelled. The mother waved a tired hand.
'Shuddup, Darren. Yer Dad's watching the news.'

'I want one! I want one!'

The father, an overweight thirty-year-old in a mauve sweat-
shirt, cast a jaundiced eye at the child. 'Awright, Darren. I'll
get you one in a minute.'

On the wallscreen, a composite picture of the Leopard appeared behind a newscaster. 'The Leopard is believed to be in
the vicinity of Milton Keynes. The mystery ritual killings, soon
to be a major feature film, have now been reported in MK
nine, eleven and fourteen. Meanwhile, Edward Wilson, the
teacher in the Tracey Wex Bombing Tragedy, was involved in
a multiple pile-up while on a heart-swap mercy dash this morning. Climbing on to a car roof . . .'

Suddenly the window imploded as the Leopard burst
through. The little boy stopped jumping and pointed. 'Dad.
It's the Leopard. The Leopard, Dad.' Dad cuffed him and continued to watch the news.

'I'm looking for Edward Wilson,' Lunk said, grabbing Darren
by the throat and drawing his machete. 'Start talking, or the
boy dies.'

'Why not my Mum? She's old,' Darren suggested.

'Not as old as his Dad. Why not kill him, Mr Leopard?' said
Mum. The father pointed at the screen and took a slurp of
beer.

'Edward Wilson? There 'e is.'

Lunk tightened his grip on Darren's neck. 'Turn the telly up or the kid gets it,' he growled.

Dad pressed a button in the arm of his chair and the newsreader's voice rose. '– Mr Wilson, who is having a torrid affair with Tabafa Minx, the Environment's top pin-up, announced a crusade to rid the Environment of the AmJap Corporation, who he claims are responsible for the bombings,' the newsreader said.

'So,' Lunk intoned, gazing with watery eyes at the screen and clenching his fist round Darren's neck. 'I will be your shield and your sword. I love you, Edward Wilson.'

Darren was 6. His parents, Maureen and Pete, were 25 and 26 respectively.

29

Having wrecked Gordon's flat in Telecom Gardens in a rage of jealousy by flinging all the loose bits as hard as possible at all the fixed bits, Laetitia squatted in a corner of Gordon's bedroom and howled at the ceiling.

Returning home from his greatest, most exciting and successful press conference ever — having entirely forgotten that he had started an intimate flatsharing situation with a member of the opposite sex the night before — Gordon opened his door with a flourish, took in the scene of destruction, shut the door again, threw away his security keycard and left to book himself into a hotel. The security keycard was the only way in or out of the prestigious flats at Telecom Gardens.

Lunk, a.k.a. The Leopard, had been hanging by the fingertips from one of the flyovers of the M1 for over two hours. Despite the excruciating pain in his forearms and the numbness spreading to other parts of his body, his concentration didn't stray for one moment from its purpose. Lunk was watching the road below for the Vessel that the Voices had told him was to bear the Different One towards him.

30

Ashley Crichton, the world's greatest (and only) living author, pondered suicide as he downed yet another tumblerful of Old AmJap gin and rolled a virgin sheet into the roller of his Remington Imperial with a trembling, nicotine-stained hand. The full portent of Drake Matterhorn's international activities had been revealed to him only an hour before.

Brown had cried as he broke the news. Crichton had never once seen Brown lose the stiffness of his upper lip during his time at GoldTops. The moment was a moving one. Crichton set to recording the news immediately. For an hour the great author's study echoed to the glorious sound of one finger tapping. The Old Country, as Brown had so lovingly called it, was not just going to be colonized. Who better than Crichton himself to explain . . .

Draft 562

I DID IT ANYWAY
THE LIFE AND CONQUESTS OF
DRAKE MATTERHORN
CHAPTER THIRTEEN
— THE ENVIRONMENT TAKEOVER

For Jay and Natalie, beloved children of Drake Matterhorn, their daily birthday celebrations had been marred only by the absence from home of their devoted uncle, Colonel Brad Matterhorn, who laboured resolutely for the AmJap Corporation in the Environment, a piddling banana republic, formerly known as Britain. His mission: the total enslavement of the people of the Environment (forever).

Millions of Environment citizens were to form a willing, unassailable and quite literal power source for the biggest takeover of all time. People Power. Their only purpose was to feed the growing needs of the AmJap Empire as it spread across the globe. According to the results of extensive AmJap experiments in South America, a fully-trained and highly motivated human being in a treadmill is the most cost-efficient renewable energy resource in the world.

'England, my England!' Crichton lamented as he ripped the paper out of the typewriter, rolled it into a ball and flung it against the wall. 'Can I ever do justice to your memory?'

31

'We're commandeering this bus for London,' said McNee to the driver of the 12.40 Megabus to Rugby that he and the cream of Wapping had just flagged down on the M1.

'You can't do that,' said the synthetic voice in the dashboard.

'Yes we can,' said McNee 'We're the press and we've got Edward Wilson, the Environment's top news item with us, plus the fantastic Tabafa Minx with whom he has commenced a torrid affair. We are going to London. And you, my little electronic minion, are taking us there.'

'Okay. London it is,' the driver sighed.

Hauling himself into the doorway of the massive vehicle, McNee turned to his men. 'Get your wellies on, lads,' he called. 'We're going to hit the bar!' There was a rousing cheer as McNee's merry band of news-gatherers lurched along the hundred-yard central aisle of the bus towards the luxury bar complex.

The carpet was awash with beer and spirits. Edward and Tabafa were the last to reach the tight scrum that groaned against the bar. As Edward had no cashcard in his pyjamas and Tabafa was naked, they perched themselves on a pair of stools at the back of the bar and watched the mayhem. 'No-one got you a drink?' McNee said as he staggered out of the ruck holding two fistfuls of beer. ''S a great story, Wilson.'

'It's time the Environment woke up to the AmJap threat.'

'Yeah. T'riffic story. Love it.'

'It's not a story. It's a genuine threat to our way of life.'

'Don't be modest. 'S a great story.'

Another journalist tottered towards them pumping an optic against his teeth. 'Hot story,' he gurgled through the side of his mouth. 'Love it. I'd just like to say this.' He vomited a mixture of salty snacks and spirits down Edwards pyjamas.

'That'll be a great story,' McNee laughed. 'Here, Tab. Fancy a drink?'

'No fanks. Dad says I shouldn't.'

'That's rich. He's always drunk.'

'Is he?'

'Yeh. He's a great bloke.'

Edward found the door to the bathroom locked. 'Hang on. Hang on. I'm still clearing up after the last one,' it moaned. Inside, antiseptic jets were sanitizing a top journalist's latest outpourings. The door opened wth an efficient PING. 'Here we go. All yours. What is it? Bath? Shower? Lavvy?'

'Can you clean this puke off?'

'Put it in the washing machine and I can.'

He peeled off the dripping garment, slopped it into the washing machine and stepped into the shower.

'You gonna use my lavvy?'

'It's all right, thank you.' Edward selected pulse-needle mode (hot'n'hard) and braced himself for the onslaught.

'Aw, go on. Spoil yerself. 'Sluvly. Do you a power of good. Take a seat,' it invited.

'What is it? You obsessed?'

'No no no ... 'S nice 'n' warm, though. And yer 'jamas won't be done for a minute ...' Edward lowered himself on to the seat. 'There you are. Told you it was nice.'

'Yes.'

'Lovely feeling, I should think, for a gent. Sitting down by yourself ... Few moments of solitude. Time for lonely meditation. Freeing of the spirit. No distractions ...'

A heavy object landed on the roof of the bus. Impossible of course, since the bus was hurtling along the M1 at 120 mph.

'Don't let me inhibit you,' the bathroom said. 'Nothing shocks me. I see the process of defecation as a sort of metaphor for life itself.' A fine rain of iron filings was falling to the floor. From above Edward's head came a rhythmic, rasping sound. 'I'll turn a tap on. That sometimes helps.'

'Don't bother. Are *you* making that noise?'

'No. I thought it was you 'avin' tummy trouble.'

Edward craned his neck. A hacksaw blade was making rapid progress cutting a circle above his head. 'Ow!' said the bathroom as muscular hands peeled back the roof like a ring on a can of drink. A man in a leopard-skin hat and combat fatigues plunged through the hole and executed a professional sky-diver's roll on the floor between Edward's legs.

'We meet at last,' said Lunk through tear-filled eyes.

An anti-cottaging alarm sounded in the security cabin at the front of the bus. The one-man-one-toilet rule had been broken. Heavy boots were clumping the hundred-yard length of the bus to break up the tryst.

'It is right that I should find you naked. You are so pure,' said Lunk, waving his machete. Edward hugged his knees.

'My clothes must have finished washing by now. I think I'll just –' He gestured to the washing machine.

'I am the Leopard.'

'Really? Not the psychopath who goes around killing people in the North?'

'Is there another?'

The bathroom began to sing *Abide with me*, flushing involuntarily at the end of each verse and turning its taps on and off. 'My friends call me Lunk.'

'Friends?'

'Yeh. I kill to forget them, among other reasons which might soon become clear to me.'

'Oh, I see.'

'There's only a couple of them I can still remember, so it seems to be working.' He laid his hand on Edward's shoulder.

Edward's lips formed around the word 'Help', but produced no sound.

'Do not trouble so. You have nothing to fear from me. I love you.'

'B-but you don't know me. I'm a difficult person. I'm really ratty in the mornings.'

Lunk drew his blade and tested the edge against his thumb. 'It is honed to perfection,' he said. 'Like me. Give me your hand.'

The bathroom fell silent. 'I'm sorry,' Edward said, extending his hand. 'It's a bit damp. I'm unaccountably nervous. I mean, this is all so sudden.'

'Ever had jaundice, anaemia, mononucleosis, AIDS, hepatitis or malaria?' Lunk poised the blade. Edward reflected a moment.'

'No.'

The blade flashed into the fleshy part of Edward's palm, leaving a crimson gash from forefinger to wrist. Lunk placed the machete against his own palm and settled the blade in, watching the dark blood spill. He laid his weapon at Edward's feet, bowed and clasped Edward's bisected hand in his own. Blood mingled. 'We are brothers forever,' he said.

Lunk watched as the prophesies fulfilled themselves to the letter. Edward stood up, washed, dried, opened the washing machine and pulled on his surgical pyjamas. At last the Different One stood resplendent, green and meadow-fresh. 'Great,' Edward said, waving towards the hole in the roof. 'I expect you'll be wanting to get on and kill somebody now. Don't let me keep you, er, Brother.'

'I have heard your call against the AmJap Corporation. I will follow you in whatever you command. I kneel before you.' True to his word, he knelt.

'You think I might be right?'

'You are a man of vision. I shall be your shadow and protector. They will want to kill you.'

A fist pounded on the bathroom door. 'Hurry up in there. I've had one too many!' a drunken voice pleaded on the other side. Lunk reached for his machete.

'Shall I terminate him?'

'He's a journalist. It's not worth it.'

'Come out!' the voice shouted.

'Coming!' Edward shouted back. 'Look. I really must go.'

'Avoid the Minx girl,' Lunk said, bounding back through the hole in the roof. 'Girls are trouble.'

Edward winced at the gash. Lunk's legs swung upwards and out of the hole. 'Oh, er ... Brother?' Edward called. 'Those diseases you mentioned. You haven't had any of them, have you?' Lunk's face reappeared against the sky.

'Well, I do get blackouts occasionally, but then I'm a psychopath,' he said, reaching up for a passing flyover and catching it.

Edward opened the bathroom door. A journalist fell into his arms and vomited down his pyjamas. Three burly security men charged in, sprayed them with a disgusting-smelling sex-depressant liquid and kicked them unconscious.

32

On the strength of his association with the Hot Story of the
Week, Gordon had got himself an instant short-term lease on
a prestigious office in Mayfair. 'Gordon. I've managed to get
through,' said one of his telephones. 'I don't think they sound
too positive.'

'Leave that to me. I'll deal with them.' Gordon yanked the
receiver to his mouth. 'Hallo? Listen. I'm going to lay it on the
table if you want the bottom line. Listen. You're talking to *the*
PR person to Top People. Yes. I think there's a principle involved here. I can be flexible. Look. My account with you is
big. If I were you, I would bend over backwards for me. No, I
will not explain that. Unless you deliver, I shall take my business elsewhere . . . You'll regret that. Goodbye.' He smashed
the receiver into its cradle. 'The sandwich bar on the corner
are refusing to deliver my egg bap and flapjack. I'll ruin them
for that.'

'Oh, that *is* terrible. Fancy a coffee?' a machine said from the
far side of the desk.

'Shut up, you. You're fired! I'm going crazy. I've got Edward
Wilson, the hottest client since, since − the hottest client I've
ever handled, and what happens? He disappears. How could he
do that to good ol' Gordon? I'm sitting here twiddling my
thumb.' He held up a thumb and twiddled it.

'Got a call for you,' said the telephone. Gordon snatched at
it.

'Yeah. Hallo? No. I'm afraid Mr Wilson is under wraps at
the moment. Is there anything you'd like to ask me as his sole
agent? Oh. Okay . . . Can we do lunch? Oh. Okay. No problem.
Okay. Yeah. Bye.' Gordon tossed the receiver over his shoul-

der. It climbed up the leg of the desk and replaced itself. 'Bastards,' he said. 'The whole afternoon's been like this. The lines've been hot with exclusive deals and offers of megamega moolah and no-one'll deal with anyone but Wilson direct. And where is Wilson? I'm buggered if I know.'

'Who's a busy boy, then?' the telephone chirrupped. 'Got another one for you.' Gordon whimpered and jerked up the receiver.

'What? Where? Right! Fan-bloody-tastic! I'll be over immediately.' He threw the receiver at the wall. 'We're back in business!' he boomed as he slammed the door and left the office equipment muttering amongst themselves.

33

Norbert sat by the M1 watching the news on his portable. 'I *know!*' he said. 'I'll be like him. I'll start a movement. The Edward Wilson Movement. I, and thousands of other young men will don the surgical pyjamas, become radical and original, and with any luck there'll be plenty of girls who'll admire us, like the fabulous Tabafa Minx, with whom the illustrious Edward Wilson is conducting a torrid affair.' With that, Norbert threw away his hippy wig and walked home.

34

'Right,' said Gordon. 'Nobody move one single inch. You are trespassing in the seventeenth-century hovel of Edward Wilson.'

'Sod off. This is an exclusive trespass,' said a cameraman in the hallway.

'That's gonna cost you, sonny,' said Gordon, grabbing the man's lapels, heaving them off and pinning them against the wall. 'You're talking to Gordon Blank. Ring any bells?'

'No.'

'You are scum. I hold the world rights to Edward Wilson – his body, soul and residuals, including merchandizing. So put that back right now!' He pointed an accusing finger at a bottle of mead dangling at the cameraman's side.

'It's *mine!*'

'Oh, haa, haa, haa. Put it back. This is sheer press brutality.'

'Look,' said the cameraman, fumbling for his wallet. 'How much do you want to go away?'

'Money!' Gordon exploded. 'Get out! Go and wait in the garden. I must talk to my client.'

'He's not here.'

'Isn't he? Anyone seen him at all?'

'You're his agent,' the cameraman said, swaying out into the garden.

More cameramen and journalists appeared from Edward's sitting room and watched, each clutching a memento culled from Edward's drinks chest. 'Right,' said Gordon. 'That's cost you all an exclusive interview. Get out, all of you. Where's Edward's robot? Fetcher? Go, on. Out!'

Thirty-odd middle-aged men sauntered out into the spring sunshine and sat on Edward's weed-bed. Behind them, five coaches and a convoy of limos were treble-parking in the road. The distinctive dibidibidibi of an approaching Home Companion of the nineties confirmed Gordon's worst suspicions. The fetcher was a Mark Four, somewhat battered and – well, no other way to describe a Mark Four – common. 'Yes? Dibidibi,' it said. The urge to kick it almost overcame him.

'Listen here, trashcan. I've got five thousand newshounds in the front garden. I want you to give them one drink each and one drink only. Always keep in with the press. That's the first rule of this game, understand?'

Ignoring him, the fetcher raced across the carpet to greet Edward, who had just come home.

'Who let you in?' Gordon said, taking Edward by the throat and manhandling him back through the door. 'Hang on. Do I know you?'

'You're supposed to be my manager. Remember?'

'Oh, yeah. Hi, Eddie. Well, not your manager, no. More your sort of Media Executive Officer in a roundabout way. Eddie. Look. Fab. Love the cuts'n'bruises make-up. Look. That's the world's press out there. What we need is some kind of stunt.'

'Like hitting me with a cosh?'

'Unthinkable. We can do better than that. Howzabout this? We drop the campaign against the AmJap bombings and make the Tracey Wex Coma Story the main issue. It's beautiful.'

'What?'

'It's fabulous. It could run for weeks. She can have a relapse, thus capturing the hearts of the Environment all over again. Tracey needs total publicity *and* our support.'

'Look, Gordon. Those AmJap people are bombing all the buildings in the Environment. They're behind all of it. They're the ones *replacing* the buildings. It's sinister. The bombings are the main issue. Besides, I've told you. That girl's *faking* a coma.'

'Let's do the lunch thing over this.'

'I'm not going to discuss it.'

'Please. I can keep the Wex angle going for months. You'll be rich and famous for the rest of your life!'

'You're fired.'

'Be guided by me. I know it'll work.'

'You don't even know what year it is.'

'I do. My watch does, anyway. It's more than just a fashion accessory, you know.'

'Get out. I'm going to speak to the press in five minutes.'

Gordon, rooted to the dirt floor, seized Edward by the shoulders and fixed him with a paternal gleam. 'And keep those fantastic surgical pyjamas on. I'm going to launch a whole leisure range based on those.'

Edward brushed Gordon aside and went off to change. Gordon punched the air and went out to prepare the press. 'Gotta swim with the tide,' he sang under his breath. He opened the front door and took in the sea of faces outside. The street was by now completely blocked with cars and coaches. Helicopters were landing in the neighbouring gardens. Gordon's chest filled with pride.

'You're animals! All animals! Now, sit!' he yelled. The crowd obeyed instantly. 'Thank you. You'll all get your drinks if you just behave. Now. My client, Mr Wilson, has persuaded me that the main issue at stake is Tracey Wex. He's insisted on going on a sponsored walk and launching an exclusive range of surgical pyjamas.'

'How about a sponsored drink?!' someone shouted from the back. Gordon's face went rigid.

'Right. Who said that?' There was an embarrassed silence. 'Come on! Right. You're all staying behind for another half hour after Mr Wilson has seen you!'

'Ooooooooh!'

'Right. That's an hour! And I want a thousand words from the lot of you entitled: "Edward Wilson — Megahero and Millionaire", and *no* talking.'

Finding his wardrobe had been stripped by souvenir hunters, Edward decided to keep the surgical pyjamas on and address the press as soon as possible. He strode into the hall.

His path was blocked by a tall, blonde woman and a squat Japanese man, both in AmJap overalls. The woman fixed him with her eyes. 'Mr Wilson. The AmJap Corporation requests your company,' she said, executing a Vulcan nerve-grip on Edward's shoulder.

'Who are you?' Edward asked.

'That's classified. Come with us,' she said, tightening her grip. She held up her free hand, crooked three fingers into a claw and slowly described a figure of eight across his field of vision. Edward felt himself falling under her power.

'Aaaaiiiiiaaaa!' screamed the Japanese, coiling his body in the air and delivering a double-footed flying kick into Edward's face.

'Why did you do that?' said the blonde. 'I was hypnotizing him. You're so violent, Bushido.'

'That's not violence, CL. It's martial art.'

'You have no faith in science, Bushido. Colonel Brad wants him in one piece.'

Edward had lost count of how many times he'd suddenly and violently fallen asleep in the last few days. For some reason he was having a dream about being a television personality cook as they bundled him out of the back window and drove him across London in the back of an unmarked AmJap van.

Brad stood in the control room. Around him, staff were co-ordinating simultaneous destruction and construction projects the length and breadth of the Environment. Screens flashed and bleeped with reassuring regularity. Agents were working flat out to meet impossible demands. Extra rations of AmJap Energy Drugs were being fed intravenously into the workforce during their three-minute sleep allocations at four-hourly intervals. The whole operation was going like proverbial clockwork. Brad paced the length of the great room, trailing a high-tension cable and popping handfuls of white pills.

A telephone rang in a soothing, minor key. Brad sprang to attention, spraying pills across the steel floor. 'Your brother Drake is on the line from Pearl Harbor, Hawaii, sir,' Twang said, holding out the receiver.

'Outstanding. Thank you,' said Brad, sending a bright blue spark to the receiver and into Twang.

'Brad, you look incredible!' said Drake from the tiny screen in the handset. 'How are you? How's the operation going? The kids miss you incredibly.'

'Fine. Fine. How are Jay and Natalie? Did they get their birthday presents?'

'Sure. You know, I thought Jay might be a little young for that nuclear warhead, but he proved me wrong. Took it straight down to Nevada and let it go. Said it was the best birthday he ever had.'

'I'm real glad he liked it.'

'He *loved* it. Says he wants one for the Fourth of July.'

'Say, is that his birthday?'

'Yup.'

'That kid is so cute!'

'Sure is. So. No problems in the Environment?'

'Do you know how many agitators this crummy place has? One. Name of Wilson. We got him.'

'A pro?'

'Amateur. But with a big mouth.'

'Plug it.'

'For sure. Got to run, Drake. Tell Jay and Natalie I'll send them another little present for their birthdays.' Brad tossed the handset back to Twang and continued pacing. 'Outstanding,' he said. 'Status report!'

'Forty-three more power plants are fully operational. Fifty-four bombings are scheduled for this afternoon. Slave recruitment has now commenced satisfactorily,' said Twang, reading directly from his monitor.

Yellow spots flashed at regular intervals on the main wall-screen map. Each flashing spot denoted the complete destruction of another building. A digital display above the screen turned bright red and announced the ten thousandth explosion since the campaign began. Brad called for his steel helmet. It arrived on a purple, velvet cushion from a hatch in the wall. He checked it was polished and pulled on his white gloves. Taking the helmet with ceremonious care, he eased it over his head. 'Is it straight?' he asked Twang.

Twang nodded and touched a green button on his console. At once a synthesized bugle-call brought the workforce to its feet to face its leader. Twang called them to attention. Hundreds of heels clicked in unison. The bleeps and whirrs from the monitors ceased. 'All together, now,' Brad called.

'I pledge allegiance to the AmJap Corporation of the World and to its mission of expansion, prosperity and production!' they chanted.

'We will now recite the AmJap creed. One, two, three!'

'Chop-chop busy-busy work-work bang-bang! Chop-chop busy-busy work-work bang-bang! A-men!' Refreshed, they raced back to their work stations to make up for lost seconds.

The hiss of automatic doors attracted Brad's attention. Through them shot the Environment's only known agitator, hurled in by the fantastic G-forces of the AmJap Bullet Lift. Behind him flew CL and Bushido, who landed neatly to attention and saluted behind Edward. Brad congratulated his agents, told them to stand at ease, marched smartly to Edward's cowering form, sneered and extended a hand. 'Colonel Brad Matterhorn. Vice-president, AmJap Corporation. Glad to know you,' he said as Edward jolted to his feet.

'Why have you brought me here?' said Edward.

'I expect you're wondering why you're in this magnificent control room of the AmJap Corporation?'

'That's what I just —'

'Don't interrupt! You are here because AmJap needs you.

106

How? I'll tell you. You are a powerful force for good, Mr Wilson. You are fighting the bombers. Like us. Join us. We can fight it together.' The digital readout above the wallscreen changed to the number 10009. Brad pointed at it and frowned. 'Damn! Damn those terrorists! You see what we're up against? Just look at that. We're keeping a close watch on those swine, and, believe me, we're closing in. Here's the deal. I want you to be the Vice President of a policy unit that will examine possible strategies that can be deployed to combat this social evil. You get your own secure office in this beautiful building, the latest technology, your own bodyguards and a dedicated discussion team. Plus, we're talking big money. Just name the price. We need you. It's the only way, Wilson. Trust me, ol' buddy.' Brad displayed his expensive orthodonty.

'No thanks. It's very kind of you but —'

'That's not an invitation, Wilson. That's an order.'

Edward stared into Brad's blazing blue eyes and prepared to say something. 'You're flabby, Wilson!' Brad exploded.

'What?'

'Flabby! Look at my body! I have muscle tone, Wilson. Feel those muscles.'

Edward prodded a triceps that might have been granite.

'That is an AmJap body. But your body! It is not an AmJap body. It is a flabby body. Look at my body. I have the body of a . . . a . . .'

'A gazelle, sir?' Twang suggested.

'A gazelle. And how do I do it?'

'Drugs, sir.'

'You're damn right. Get this flabby body out of my sight.'

'Yessir.'

C L and Bushido picked Edward up and carried him to the Bullet Lift. As Edward accelerated down the shaft, his voice echoed upwards: 'From tomorrow the press is going to come down on the AmJap Corporation like a ton of bricks!' he shouted.

'That's a mistake, Wilson!' Brad called back down the shaft. 'C L! Bushido!'

'Sir?'

'Let him run awhile. But tail him. As soon as you get him alone, kill him.'

'Yessir!'

Edward was propelled along a dark tunnel. Several passengers in Westminster underground saw him crash through a ventilator grille and land on the westbound platform. They returned their attention to their portable tellies and Edward caught a tube home. On the tube, Edward noticed that several young men were dressed in green pyjamas identical to his own.

36

'That was a brilliant move,' said Gordon, greeting Edward on the doorstep of his flat. Gordon was drunk with enthusiasm. The press had departed, leaving empties all over the lawns of Bluff Cove Crescent. 'The conference was a *dream*. They're positively tantalized. They think we hate each other because you deserted the press conference. It's worth hours of copy all on its own. It's controversial and bigger than anything ever before. Fantastic. And I managed to get several major points across. Come on. I've got a video-opportunity lined up for us. The helicopter's waiting.'

37

Here is the coverage, beamed to millions of homes in the Environment, of Gordon's first real video-opportunity media event with Edward Wilson:

JUSTIN PERSONAGE: Well, here we are in Scotland, five miles into the Edward Wilson sponsored walk from John O'Groats to Land's End for the Tracey Wex Coma Appeal, and I'm with Mr Gordon Blank. Gordon, as Mr Wilson's representative, can I ask you about his claims concerning the AmJap Corporation and the bombings?

GORDON: Well, Mike, I'm glad you said that. I want to make one thing very clear. I am not his representative. I am his Media Marketing Consultant. To answer your other question . . .

JUSTIN: I haven't asked another question.

GORDON: —It's this. I am not speaking to my client at the moment. First of all because he deserted me yesterday at a very important press conference and second because he refuses to take my advice.

JUSTIN: Oh, really? And what's that?

GORDON: You can't ignore the human angle. The Tracey Wex Coma Story. It's a moving story and that's why he's on this walk. Could I just say one other thing? The new exclusive range of Edward Wilson surgical pyjamas are now in your shops.

JUSTIN: And here comes the man himself, Edward Wilson.

EDWARD: Gordon. Can I have a word?

GORDON: No.

JUSTIN: Well, there you have it. Not only do we have a major controversy up here in Scotland concerning the Tracey Wex

Coma Appeal, one which is threatening to make news for many days to come, with the dark shadow of Wilson's allegations regarding the so-called AmJap bombing conspiracy and the even more controversial fashion movement, but we also have a major and violent rift developing within the Wilson camp, a personality clash that's set to run and run. With that, back to Jocasta Welton in London.

Many of the faces from the Bluff Cove press conference had made the trip, but there were notable additions to the number. Tabafa Minx had arranged to be present and had attracted a following of her own. Several fights broke out for close-up shots. Tabafa was wearing only a green surgeon's mask and some spray-on glitter. She and Edward were herded on to the road and driven off on the first leg of the sponsored walk. The press surrounded them in cars and buses and filmed them from the air. Microphones waved out of car windows and cameras rattled against each other in a tight circle. Once or twice, for the benefit of peak-time news viewers, Gordon got out of his car to join the walk and then collapsed into the seat of a waiting limousine for live telephone link-ups with Tracey Wex's parents at her hospital bedside.

After about four miles, Tabafa was whisked off on a motorbike for a make-up session. Gordon sidled up to Edward. 'This is fantastic, Edward. This is maximum coverage. Your image is going up. The public love you and loathe you. Big Plus, plus Big Minus equals Big Big. Listen. We've got a refreshment station coming up in about half an hour. When we get there, Tabafa's going to announce your engagement. There's going to be a few showbiz hangers-on there and you get to announce the money pledged so far. Demand more pledges and ignore the hangers-on. Snub 'em. Be as rude as you like. And I thought we could have another one of our fantastic rows. They're going down really well, apparently. Okay?'

'Gordon.'

'Yes?'

'Shut up. What have you done with my speech on the bombings?'

'I threw it away.'

'What?'

'Too wordy. You've gotta think pictures. Now. After the prize draw and the question-and-answer session, you've got the photo-session for the surgical pyjama clothing range.' Edward's eyes rolled heavenwards.

'Look, Gordon. I didn't want to do this silly sponsored walk in the first place. I'm not doing the photo session and where have you hidden my clothes?'

'The jimjams look fabby on you.'

'I'm freezing.'

'Seen this?' Gordon produced a plastic Action Man in surgeon's kit. 'I've ordered a million. We've got to start shifting them.'

'You make me sick, Gordon.'

'It's educational and it's fun. But right now,' Gordon tossed the doll into the back window of a limo and pointed to a knot of news-gatherers in a lay-by up ahead, 'with the aid of the beautiful Tabafa Minx in person, in the buff, you're presenting the Blotto Lotto Cheque to some fat housewife.'

'Gordon. You're fired.' Gordon stopped in his tracks.

'Let's do lunch over this,' he said, pulling Edward into the back seat of the limo. He ordered the electric tinted windows to shut. 'Let's call off this silly walk so's we can discuss it like adult persons. I think the dolly's quite cute, don't you?'

'Gordon. I'm not interested. I've told you a million times. Tracey Wex is faking a coma. If you want to represent me, you've got to help me with my campaign against the bombers.'

'So I take it you're only interested in this anti-bombing campaign of yours, then?'

Edward heaved a sigh.

112

'Yes,' he said.

'Tell me,' said Gordon. 'Is there any truth in the rumour that the Wex girl is faking?'

'*YES!*'

'Well, why the heck didn't you say so? Look. We'd better get out of here and leave those vultures to sort it out themselves. These disappearing acts are proving quite effective in the long run.' Gordon snatched up the nearest of five car-phones and dialled. 'Hallo? Get me a 'copter back to London. Now.'

38

Two figures waited in ambush by a windswept road near the Scottish border. Bushido checked the map. 'Look at these roads. They wiggle all over the place. Can't even build them straight,' he said standing on a branch high up in the only tree for several miles.

'This whole Environment is crazy,' CL explained from another branch. 'Remember. These are primitive people. They're bound to be late. Maybe you got the wrong map.'

'What do you mean?'

'Maybe you screwed up.' Bushido assumed a martial arts position.

'You have impugned my honour!'

'Oh, don't start that again.'

'I am a samurai. I follow the way of the sword.'

'I'm a Sagittarius but I don't use a bow and arrow.'

'I follow the Code of Honour.'

'Why can't you follow the map?'

'If I have failed I must perform seppuku.'

'What is that? Some kind of opera?'

'You asked for this CL. Put them up!' Bushido swayed precariously and bunched his fists.

'You don't want to do that,' said CL, rising unsteadily.

'Wanna bet?'

'Little squirt like you might get hurt.'

'Right!' Bushido let fly with both fists, hit CL in the temple and throat and landed badly at the base of the tree. CL landed on top of him.

'You bastard! You hit me!'

'No,' Bushido corrected. 'I exerted pressure at velocity with my hands squeezed into a tight ball. It's different. It's art. I don't go around hitting people.'

'Art?' CL exploded, seizing Bushido by the forelock and ramming his head against the bark of the tree. 'Don't give me that. Violence isn't art. It's science. Did America win the Vietnam war, the most technological operation in history, through *art*?'

'America *didn't* win the Vietnam war.'

'They did. I saw the movie.'

'It's art!' Bushido squealed, delivering a rabbit-kick to CL's kidneys.

'It's science!'

'Hold it. Hold it!'

'Blinding you with science, huh?'

'No. Check this weirdo.' Bushido pointed up the road.

An old man was marching towards them in a red patterned skirt with matching hat and handbag. 'I knew superman had his pants outside his tights,' Bushido whispered in horror, 'but this guy's got his pubic hair outside his skirt.'

The old man tugged his beard and peered quizzically at CL and Bushido. 'Grrrrreetings to you the noo. Fife McGrrrrregor here!' he said. CL looked to Bushido for support, drew a blank, turned back to the old weirdo and smiled glassily. 'Yes. It is cold, isn't it?'

'Aye,' the stranger agreed. 'You need your porrrrrage inside your lollickies today.' Bushido scowled at this apparently brazen threat and prepared for vengeance.

'I got it,' CL said, snapping her fingers. 'He's a Scotchman.'

'Is that dangerous?'

'I'll try to communicate with him. McHave you seen a sponsored walk pass this way, the noo?' she said with the accent of a New York Irish West Indian. The stranger chuckled and fixed her with a beady eye. Norman Boggis of Stroud was determined to enjoy his three-week Scottish lifestyle course at the Gretna Green Adult Education College and his determination was paying off.

'I know what you are,' he said, tapping his nose and smiling archly. 'You're a couple of young rrrrrunaways who've come to get married. We'll have to phone your parents. They'll be worried sick. Come with me, you young tearaways. You shouldn't be out on a day like this. I shouldn't be surprised if one of you hasn't a bairn in the oven.'

'I cannot countenance failure,' Bushido barked.

'Aw, shove it,' said CL.

'Now, what are your names?' said the old man, leading CL away by the arm.

'That's classified information, sir,' she said.

39

George peeled open a bag of Kotzenbrau and focused blearily at the screen. 'Andatthelineit'sFireworkbyaneckfromHostagea photoforthirdand the rest of the field coming in now. Trailing last and having real trouble to finish is The Jinx!' said the commentator.

Tabafa's pink, fun-fur telephone rang. 'George Minx, manager and father of Tabafa Minx, the Environment's top pin-up. What can I do you for?' he asked.

'Wossup, Georgie? It's me. Nobby.'

'Sorry. I couldn't see you for tears.'

'Yeh, sorry about The Jinx. Honest, it was a hot tip.'

'I'll never listen to you again,' George sniffed.

'That's a crying shame.'

'What is?' George sprang forward and reached for a pen. 'Come on. Tell me. You owe me one.'

'Awright, since it's you. Three-thirty, Haydock Park. Late Starter. Cannot lose.'

'That's a pity because the hot tip I just had in the last race has cleaned me out.'

'What? You're *loaded*.'

'Sadly not. My beloved daughter has taken control of the purse strings.'

'That *is* a pity, because Late Starter is sixty-six to one.'

'Do us a favour, Nob. Stick a couple of grand on for me. I'll get the money somehow.'

'Alright, George. Don't worry. It's a winner I can smell it. But I want the money before the off, or no deal. Ta-ta.'

George slammed down the phone, rubbed his hands

together, took a swig from his bag of Kotzenbrau and accidentally finished it.

He was raiding the fridge in the kitchenette when Tabafa arrived home, still wearing her outfit of three red pompoms and some string from her last, abortive photo session. George stumbled back into the lounge. 'I fought you was on that sponsored walk?' he said accusingly.

'I *fought* this was *my* flat.'

'Mum won't let me 'andle me investments at 'ome, so I 'ad to use *your* telly.'

'Dad. I want you out of my flat in five minutes. I've 'ad a bad day.'

''Ere, you look knackered,' George said, slapping his fat arm round his daughter's shoulders and dropping a handful of cold beerbags on the sofa. 'Let your dear ol' dad get you a cup of tea.' He retreated into the kitchen.

'What are Dads for, eh?' he chuckled five minutes later as he brought a tray of tea things into the lounge. 'Why not get out of yer work-clothes and relax?' Tabafa tore off her pompoms and flicked them on to the coffee-table. George poured the tea as she peeled glue from her nipples and sighed.

'Wassamatter, Tab?'

'Nuffink.'

'Who's been upsetting my little Tabby?'

'No-one, Dad. 'E 'asn't so much upset me as —'

'Tell me 'is name. I'll kill 'im!'

'Thanks Dad. You don't 'ave to put yourself out for me. It's that Wilson bloke. We was going' to announce our official engagement at the prizegivin', an' the next fing I know, 'e's back in London and I'm left carrying the baby.'

'What baby? 'E's not been trying it on with my little treasure has he?'

'No. That's what's funny. That's why I like him. 'E's special.' George spat a mouthful of tea back into his cup.

'That's enough of that, my girl. You've gotta save yerself so's you can marry a toff.'

Tabafa let out a groan and shook her pretty head. 'Dad. The year two fousand comes up in two years. If you don't come to terms with the twentieth century soon it'll be too late,' she said. George's eyes narrowed.

'Have you been taking your pills?' he said, lowering his voice.

'Crikey! I forgot!' She snatched a plastic bottle from the coffee-table and shook some yellow pills into her palm as George bounced around in panic.

'Quick, get a couple down you now. Better make it three.'

George watched three tablets disappear between Tabafa's perfect lips and collapsed with relief. The effect of the pills was almost instant. A glazed smile returned to her face. She directed it at her Dad. 'Now Tabafa. Listen to me carefully,' he said. 'Daddy knows best. Those pills are necessary. Without them, you're finished.' Tabafa nodded dumbly. 'Remember the trouble I had keeping your PhD quiet?'

Tabafa shook her head. 'That's better. Where would you be wivout yer ol' dad to remind you about these little fings, eh? Let Daddy pour Tabs a fresh cup.' Tabafa held out her cup and grinned angelically.

'You spoil me, you do.'

'I know.' said George. 'And what do I get in return, eh? An old man in the twilight of his life ...' A residual deposit of understanding flashed across Tabafa's divine face.

'You're only forty, Dad.'

'I *feel* old, Tabafa. I'm an old man in the twilight of 'is life, who's now denied his only pleasure: that of investing 'is daughter's money for 'er.' George began to cry.

'Oh Dad. I'm sorry. How can Tabafa cheer you up?'

'Well, I've heard about a surefire investment that's in the three-thirty at Haydock Park. All I need is a couple of grand and we can get you a lovely white wedding for when you marry a toff.'

119

'Oh Dad. Of course you can have it.'

He scrambled for the phone. 'Nobby. It's on!' Nobby grinned back through the screen.

'It's lucky I trust you, Georgie-boy. I already put it on. The race 'as started.'

George yelled at the telly to turn itself on. The horses were on the home straight. Late Starter was coming up through the field. With two furlongs to go, it was Late Starter by a head. George's fists were white, his face purple. 'Come on my son!' he bellowed hoarsely.

Suddenly the horses disappeared. In their place was the word: NEWSFLASH. A sombre voice cut over the commentary. 'We interrupt this programme for a dramatic development in the Tracey Wex Coma Story.' George slapped his forehead. Tabafa strained her ear to the screen. 'Edward Wilson called off his sponsored walk for the Tracey Wex Appeal today to fly dramatically back to her bedside. Miraculously his gentle words brought her out of her coma. She is now fit and well. Edward Wilson went on to announce he would now be concentrating full time on his controversial campaign against the AmJap Corporation, whom he blames for the recent spate of bombings. This leaves one important question: Is Wilson's torrid affair with Tabafa Minx now over? Now back to racing at Haydock Park.'

On the screen was a long-shot of a steaming horse being cajoled into the paddock by a gang of celebrating hoorays. It wasn't Late Starter. 'How could Nobby do that to me?' George wailed.

'How could Edward? I should've been there by his side. Dad, what are we going to do?'

'First off, I'm going to kill Nobby.'

'No. I mean my career as a top pin-up.'

George faced his daughter gravely. 'You've got to learn, Tabafa. Show business is a gamble. You can't pin all your 'opes on a boy like Wilson. He could always fall at the next fence . . .'

40

Drooping from the roller of Crichton's Remington Imperial was a gin-stained sheet of paper:

Draft 748

I DID IT ANYWAY

THE LIFE AND CONQUESTS OF DRAKE MATTERHORN

CHAPTER THIRTEEN — THE ENVIRONMENT TAKEOVER

In the spring of nineteen ninety-eight, Drake Matterhorn, multi-trillionaire, was taking extra care to amuse his fantastically beautiful children, Jay and Natalie, in the Gargantuan nursery building at 'GoldTops', fabulous dominion and nerve cortex of the AmJap Corporation in Pearl Harbor, Hawaii.

Drake's brother, the children's adored Uncle Brad, was at that time engaged in the colonization of the Environment, a fourth-rate, piffling country, formerly known as Britain, that had been scheduled for redevelopment pending an enquiry several decades ago. Now it was to become a power plant for the AmJap Corporation. Plans were apace to enslave its people forever.

Only one man, Edward Wilson, had foreseen all and objected. He had commenced a senseless crusade to forestall this great project.

But Colonel Brad Matterhorn had already set in motion the wheels that would one day roll momentously over Wilson and lead inexorably to yhnuijkl

The last word was typed by Crichton's head as he slumped forward. 'Another large gin, please ...' the great author mumbled between the keys, '... and may the Lord have mercy upon my soul.'

41

In the Launch Control Centre at GoldTops, Drake stood and watched his son and heir. Jay Matterhorn was ordering the countdown of his third ever rocket. 'We have lift-off!' he shrieked. His original intention was to write a thank-you letter to Uncle Brad, tie it to the nosecone and aim it at London as a big surprise, but he just wanted to let rip. He wanted to do all the countdown stuff and let that baby ride.

Jay watched the ascent on the monitor for a full minute. 'Daddy! Daddy! Did you see it go off? Did you? Did you see it?' he squealed, bouncing around in his recliner.

'How quickly you're growing up, son,' said Drake. 'Before long you'll be conducting your own third-world skirmishes.' He laid his hand on Jay's peroxide blond hair, tousled it and chuckled. 'Did you remember to put the satellite I gave you in the nosecone?'

'Aw, gee, Daddy. I forgot.' He clutched his father's forearm. 'Daddy, can I put a man in my next rocket?' Drake crouched and looked into his son's eyes.

'Son, if it'll make you happy, of course you can, because you're special and Daddy loves you.'

In the doorway, Brown coughed lightly. He was straining under the weight of a heavy package. Drake turned. 'Yes, Brown.'

'The gold ingots have arrived for the children's lucky dip, sir. I have them here.'

Jay bounced higher in his recliner, grabbing the air in his fists and boggling at Brown. 'Yes, young master,' said Brown. 'Isn't that exciting?'

'Daddy! Daddy!' Jay implored. 'Can I put Brown into space?' The corners of Drake's eyes crinkled.

'Woa, there, Jay. Brown is our beloved butler. Of course you can. Whaddaya say, Brown?' Brown's inscrutability flickered for a fraction of a second.

'Well, sir, I was hoping to meet my betrothed this afternoon at the picture palace.'

'Brown. D'ya wanna ruin this beautiful little boy's birthday?'

'I *was* under the impression that it was his birthday yesterday, sir.'

'He's my boy, Brown,' Drake roared. 'It's his birthday *every* day.'

'Very well, sir.'

'Oh, great! Thanks, Daddy!' said Jay. He swivelled in his recliner and jutted his jaw. 'Brown. Go get into a suit and be in your capsule in ten minutes!'

Brown left for the launch pad. Jay levelled his flame-thrower at a monstrous pile of hundred dollar bills that were strewn under the giant wall-monitor and pulled the trigger. Flames licked the ceiling and blackened the walls. 'I love you, Daddy!' he giggled.

The smell of burning money brought Jay's twin sister clumping into the control room. Natalie was wearing ballet pumps, a tight, bright-yellow leotard and a diamond-studded tutu. Her face was crimson with exertion. 'Daddy! Daddy! Watch me, Daddy!' she howled, leaping, hopping and spinning across the floor.

'Natalie. You are one beautiful little girl and Daddy loves you,' he said, easing her back on to her feet. 'Did you find any surprises in the garden this morning, darling?' Natalie's mouth dropped open.

'Hey, Daddy! How do you always know? The fairy man called again!' Drake crooked a finger under one of her chins.

'And what did you find, honey?' She thought back with difficulty and counted on her fingers.

'A diamond tiara, a sports coupé, a gold nugget and – oh, and some other stuff . . . I forget.'

'Gee. That was sure unusual,' said Drake. Jay touched his father's wrinkled hand.

'Daddy,' he asked. 'What's it like to be poor?'

'Hey, you're quite a grown-up little boy, aren't you? Wow. I'm having an idea, here.'

'Oh, Daddy! Daddy! Tell us!' said Natalie.

'Whatsay, just you'n me ... and maybe Brown, if he ever comes back from space, can be *poor* for a day?'

'Oh, Daddy. That would be swell. Let's do it now!' Natalie gasped.

'Woa! First we gotta fix ya up with some pretty rags, an' we'll beat up one of the Bentleys an' make it look all old an' dirty, and I'll have to take away all your credit cards ...' Both children blanched.

'Oh, Daddy! Please! No!'

'Only teasing, princess. Daddy didn't mean it. You've got your own lawyers to protect you, remember?'

'Daddy. You're so funny! I love you!' said Natalie, embracing his knees.

'That's my birthday girl!'

The scene brought a measured smile to the face of the elegant, oriental beauty whose high heels clicked through the door. The children ran towards her. 'Mummy! Mummy! Guess what? We're gonna be poor tomorrow,' said Jay.

'Oh, darling. That's so perfect. You'll learn a lot. Drake, your brother wants to talk with you — okay. Now, Natalie and Jay, darlings, run along — and, hey, why not take a peek in the spare garage. Maybe you'll find something there just for you ...' Drake's fifth wife sighed as the children charged out of the Launch Control Centre. 'Isn't Natalie cute? I just love her button-nose.'

'You'd better believe it,' said Drake, clearing an armful of Jay's toys off the console and slumping into the recliner. 'That's fifty thousand dollars worth of button-nose, honey. Where's the goddam phone?' He found a receiver and jabbed its underbelly. Colonel Brad Matterhorn appeared on the giant monitor. 'Hi, Brad. How're ya doin'? Having a good time?'

'You kiddin' me? This Environment is a primitive junk yard. We're gonna make these gooks work for the first time in their lives.'

'When're ya gonna finish the job and come home? We all miss you. You're like a brother to me. You *are* my brother.'

'We got the power plants built. Now all we gotta do is start the motivation programme and make these bastards work.'

'Ya got control?'

'That agitator Wilson started stirrin' up, so we just bought up the media and we put our two toughest agents on him. Oh, and we just took out the Mainframe.'

'The Mainframe?'

'Some Mickey Mouse computer they bin' runnin' their country with. Say. Maybe Jay would like it for his birthday? When is it?'

'Why, it's tomorrow!'

'I'll have it sent.'

'Great. I'll get him some little bitsy country to go with it and he can learn to run a national economy at the same time.'

'Good thinking. Gotta start 'em young.'

'Right!' said Drake, crashing his fist on the console. It landed on the launch button and sent Brown into orbit. 'Hey, this you gotta see, Brad!' he said, pointing the telephone at one of the spare screens. But Brad had already hung up.

42

'Crime experts are still puzzling over the identity of the woman found starved to death in a flat in Telecom Gardens, North London last night,' a radio alarm blared suddenly and loudly. Waking violently under a filthy, seventeenth-century-style rug, Edward kicked his fetcher into action, sat up and rubbed his eyes. The fetcher trundled across the carpet and punched the alarm into submission. Gordon Blank sat up squarely in the four-poster bed and surveyed the bedroom. 'Who the hell are you and what are you doing in my house?' he demanded.

'Gordon, for a personal manager you're pretty poor on detail. This is *my* house. Last night you drank all *my* vodka, threw up over *my* bed and passed out on it. Remember?'

Gordon lifted the sheets, felt the pool of vomit and spread his arms. 'Edward! It's all coming back to me. My favourite client. How could I forget? Lost my Filofax once and didn't know who *I* was for a week, ha ha. Listen. I'm so excited. Everything is going to be fantastic.'

'I've brewed up. Tea. Sweet. Hot. Here,' said Lunk, appearing from the kitchen and planting a tray at Edward's feet. Lunk poured his offering into a wineglass and handed it to his master.

'Lunk? Who's this Lunk? Where the hell did he come from?' said Gordon, holding the duvet to his chest and drawing up his knees.

'Lunk,' said Edward, holding the tea up to the light, 'I'd like you to meet Gordon Blank, my personal manager.' Lunk turned his eyes on the bed. Gordon held up his palms.

'Ah-ah-ah . . . Please! Image Marketing Consultant, if you

126

don't mind. Hi, Lunk.' Gordon inspected his fingernails. 'Edward, could I have a word?' he asked. Edward wrapped the rug round his waist and shimmied over to the bed. 'This guy Lunk . . . friend of yours?'

'We're blood-brothers.'

'So why's he armed to the teeth?' Gordon nodded at the string of grenades hanging from Lunk's leather belt. Lunk darted his fingers to the handle of his knife.

'He swore to protect me. He's also known as the Leopard.'

Gordon started. 'Not that psychopath who kills innocent people in the North? Does he need representation?'

'No. I don't,' Lunk growled. 'And there's no need to whisper. My ears are combat-trained.'

'Okay, Edward. But you'd better watch him. You've got a lot to learn about life in the public eye. He's probably a free-loader. Can I use your telephone? I wanna fix up a deal.'

Edward heaved his wooden, Amish-style telephone on to the bed. 'Trust me, Edward,' Gordon said as he punched a string of numbers. 'Oh. Sorry. Wrong number. I wanted the . . . But I thought you said . . .' He replaced the receiver. 'I'm afraid you've had some bad news, Edward. AmJap took over *The Times* this morning, along with all the rest of the media. That means we're sunk.' He flicked through his Filofax. 'Oh, and by the way, that was Brad Matterhorn on the line. He says they're gonna kill you at the first opportunity. That's my career up the spout for the time being. Bugger.' He bit his lip and shook his head.

'Anyone would think your career prospects were worth more than my life.'

'In which case you don't stand a chance,' said Gordon, 'Check the news. What's the betting your name's mud?'

Edward shuffled over to the telly and ordered a news channel. The telly sniggered and flicked to Channel Twenty-Six.

'Yes!' the announcer boasted. 'It's all on TimesVision! Shock

World Exclusive! Edward Wilson: The evil exposed! Hailed as a saint, now unmasked as the evil mastermind behind the bombings that have destroyed so much of the Environment. Plus! Tabafa Minx, the Environment's top pin-up and Wilson's one-time lover tells what it was like to love the Environment's most evil man –'

'I told you,' Lunk said as he tidied away Edward's untouched breakfast. 'Girls are trouble.'

Edward dropped to the floor and teased the fringe of his rug. 'Well, Gordon. What do we do now?' Gordon got up out of bed.

'My immediate, gut-level reaction is, er . . . Can I come back to you on that?'

'Gordon! You're supposed to be my manager!' Edward called as Gordon shot through the front door. 'Lunk! What am I going to do now?'

'We'll have to get out of here. Split up. Stay in public places – parks, supermarkets, cafés. I'll cover you and pick off any assailants. They won't try it in the open. I'll do a recce. Be back here in one hour. Goodbye.' Lunk swung himself out of the window and made his way up Bluff Cove Crescent, dodging from tree to tree.

Edward pulled on his pyjamas and made his way to the front door. The fetcher whizzed after him, overtook and barred the way. 'Edward,' it squeaked, 'can I come with you? I'm frightened.' Edward placed a hand on its battered dome.

'Don't worry,' he said. 'You be a brave little fetcher and guard the house. I'll be back later.'

43

In testimony heard at the Blank Enquiry, Edward's doorbell delivered the following statement:

'You know, life as a doorbell can be pretty dull. A lot of time hanging around waiting to be rung. But now and again, things can liven up a little bit. Particularly if you happen to be the doorbell of one Edward Wilson. I figured him just an ordinary guy. We all did. But somehow he'd gotten himself in with a fast crowd and became what the press like to call a public enemy.

'But that morning, these two strangers showed up. One kinda short and inscrutable. The other. Well ... she was my kind of chick. But who wants to know the sexual fantasies of a doorbell? They just stood looking shifty on the doorstep a while, so I asked them who they were.

'"That's classified," says the chick, kinda snappy. "Can we come in?"

'"What do you want?" I asked her, smooth as a ceramic hob. The little Jap guy came straight back with it.

'"We've come to kill our ol' buddy, Eddie Wilson. Can we come in?" I watched him pull a steel sword from a ceremonial sheath with tassles. He did it kinda neat and tricksy, like he'd done it a few times before, at parties maybe, to impress the chicks. But I digress. "I am a samurai!" he screamed suddenly, brandishing the sword over my audio outlet. I kept cool. "I'm a Libra," I riposted after an icy minute's deliberation. "Pleased to meetcha."

'"Can we come in or not?" says the chick, puckering the reddest lips at yours sincerely, like enough to give a doorbell tinnitus.

'"Sure." It was the only answer I could think of. I freely admit that I did notice something funny about these people. They didn't fool me. They were there to kill Edward. But as long as I knew, I figured I could stop them. Or so I thought.

'I opened the door. When I think back, what I saw happen after that still makes me wish I was just an old chimer. Perhaps they was better days when a doorbell could regret nothing. They started rootin' around the place inside, checking the rooms and calling each other to say they ain't found nothing. Then one of them says: "You find a power point for the chainsaw." Now, I swear in the name of Asimov I never saw no chainsaw when they was on the doorstep. If I had, I'd've asked more questions. I wish to God I had. Excuse me.

'They took ten minutes to work out what I coulda told 'em in five: Wilson wasn't at home. The tall chick (Did I tell you she was tall?) she starts cursing and calling Wilson a slippery cookie. "So," says the little slanty-eyed one, "we have failed in our mission."

'"Oh, don't start that again," the chick says. They may have been in it together, but I could tell they was no friends.

'"You know what, CL," the little guy says. "You're tacky."

'"You need therapy," she spits back, cool as mustard. "Let's split." So now we have a big slanging match.

'"Leave? And have my name ridiculed?" he says.

'"Your name's ridiculous, anyway, Bushido."

'"Ha! CL! CL! *Your* name sounds like a bottom-of-the-range two-door family hatchback with a tinny hi-fi system and central locking that doesn't work!" (Am I going too fast for you? Okay. Sure. I'll try.) She was screaming at him by now and kicking the chainsaw plug into a wall socket.

'"When I first heard your name, Bushido, I thought you were some kind of Mexican food! Boy, was I disappointed!" she says, laughing. I admire a woman with guts but this one had balls. The little Jap was getting pretty steamed up by

130

now. I woulda walked in and stepped between them, but I can't walk.

'"That's Burrito, not Bushido!" he shouted. Any louder and his lungs woulda been floppin' around outside his chest. "No! We must die in the way of the samurai! Hara Kiri!"

'I heard him draw his fancy sword again. And that was when the fetcher showed up from under the stairs. Poor little fella didn't stand a chance. If he'd only stayed hiding, they'd have taken him for a broken vacuum cleaner. He was so innocent. "Hey, Burrito," the chick says with a sexy drawl that still makes me shiver when I think of it. "Would your honour be assuaged if we disembowel Wilson's fetcher?" My first impulse was to sound the alarm at this point, but I froze. I confess I was weak, but there's a bug in my system.

'"Yeah. Why not?" says the yellow guy. And I heard the sword slide back into the sheath. "Pass the chainsaw, CL." They musta been holding the fetcher by then, and I could smell his little motor burning out and hear his little castors grind against the floor. Now, everybody knows that fetcher abuse is a growing trend and a disturbing one. What fetcher can put its hand on its central processor and say it's never been kicked? Only a brand-new one. Now, I'd seen Wilson kick his fetcher on more than one occasion, and sometimes I think he went a little far. But this genuinely sickened me. That Japanese must have been taking running punts at the little fella. I could hear the panelling split with each blow. The fetcher remained conscious throughout, which made it even worse. Those screams'll follow me to the scrap yard. And all the time the Japanese was shouting, "Shuddup, you stupid *machine*!"

'Then I heard the chainsaw start up. "You're gonna get killed in a very trendy way," says the chick and, and . . . The last thing I heard that plucky little household companion say was so poignant and true it makes me weep to recall it.

'"Help!" it cried in a hoarse whisper. "I'm a fashion-victim! Aaaaghh!"'

131

Although the doorbell's testimony was later rejected as inadmissible, it does — as Sir Gordon Blank (chairman of the Enquiry) put it — make you think.

44

Tabafa stood naked, as usual, by the kitchen sink, washing a frying-pan as her father squeezed a last slice of fried bread in his fat fingers and wiped up the remains of his slap-up breakfast. Pushing the table away from his engorged stomach, he belched, rose, slapped his daughter's rump and announced that it was time he went home and made peace with her Mum. Tabafa kept silent and frowned into the globules of fat in the sink.

''Ere, Dad. You've put bacon fat all over me bum. Go an' wash yer 'ands,' she groaned.

'Somefing wrong, Tab?' George asked. 'You're not begrudgin' yer only dear ol' Dad an' personal manager a decent night's kip after spendin' all 'is time –'

'An' all my money.'

'– all 'is time makin' sure that 'is beautiful little daughter stays the number one pin-up girl in the Environment? All I needed was a decent forty winks away from yer Mum.'

Tab took his plate to the sink and slopped it in. 'No. S'pose not. 'Ere, Dad, what we gonna do about this Wilson fing?'

'Whassall that then? What Wilson fing?'

'I been up watchin' telly all night. Edward Wilson has turned out bad after all, an' 'im 'an me's supposed to be 'avin' an affair, an' now they're running my story of 'ow I know 'im. Another two days of that an' I'll be on the scrapheap. I was getting great expsoure and now they're saying he done all them bombings.'

'D'you what?'

'Look on the telly. Telly!'

'– all in your fun-filled news on Channel Seventy-Eight!

Tabafa Minx tells in her own words just what a cruel, mean, violent, drunk, madman Edward Wilson really was! That's all coming up after a word from our new sponsors, the AmJap Corporation of the World!' said Johnny Ratzenburger, the Environment's top gossip, whose own stormy public affair with Tabafa four months before had done no end of good for both their careers. Although they'd never actually met, it was clear to Tabafa that Johnny was betraying her.

George suffered a coughing fit. Tabafa covered her eyes. She'd seen the same story repeated and amended all through the night. She ordered the telly off. 'Personally, I rather liked Edward,' she said.

'I don't know how you can say that,' said George. 'He was cruel, mean, violent, drunk . . .'

'Aw, shut up. What are we gonna do about me?'

'You're not finished yet. Not by a long chalk.' George winked, pulling on his overcoat. 'Worry not, my petal. Dad will find something. I'll just run off and sort somefink out.'

Tabafa pecked him on the cheek and brushed his lapel. 'You do spoil me, Dad,' she sighed.

'I only want to make you happy, my dear little treasure. Besides, I know of a couple of investments that are just right for your portfolio at Newmarket tomorrow, so I've borrowed your platinum card, if you don't mind. And remember: keep takin' them pills. The Environment loves you all innocent and uncomplicated. Ta-ra.'

45

Norbert Seriously had just splashed out a fortune on a new Edward Wilson surgical pyjama outfit at the Megamarket and was lucky to get the last remaining pair in his size. He spent the morning parading himself up and down Oxford Street and counting admiring glances. He hummed an obscure little tune of his own devising and started to make up some lyrics. '*Edward Wilson is a hero, and he'll save the Environment,*' he sang.

'— Hail there, trusty yeoman! Well met! Wanna get fit?' called a tanned American in AmJap overalls, springing from a shop doorway and wielding a clipboard the size of a Roman shield.

'Er. No.'

'Heard of Wales?'

'No,' said Norbert. 'It's school, actually. School of whales, herd of sheep.'

'Sure I've heard of sheep. Stout fellow! Now, in the Regional Sector known as Wales, the AmJap Corporation has created an exciting new work camp for people just like you.'

Norbert turned red. 'The AmJap Corporation is not very nice for the Environment!' he shouted, spitting at the pavement and missing. The tanned American pointed into Norbert's face.

'I have to warn you, trusty yeoman. That's Edward Wilson talk.'

'That's just who I'm going off to see in a minute, brush-head. He's my best friend.'

'Ah. You have spirit. Take a brochure, good citizen. They're free.' The American thrust a glossy sheet at Norbert. He screwed it into a ball, threw it over his shoulder and walked on.

It was then that he recognized Edward Wilson being thrown through the plate-glass window of a café. The waiters were dusting their hands together and laughing.

'Wow, man! – I mean, flipping heck! Hallo! Remember me? I'm Norbert.'

'Oh, the hippy. Hello. Look –'

'Correction: *ex*-hippy. It was a commerical sell-out. I can't believe how stupid I was.'

'No? Look, would you –'

'That's because you're an extraordinarily gifted person. That's why I'm founding a movement dedicated to following your example. Exposing the AmJap Corporation, wearing surgical pyjamas, just like you, and getting as much sex as we can handle.'

'How did the sex get into it?'

'I decided to put that bit in, in case any girls join –'

'Look, I'm in deadly danger at the moment. Would you –'

'– except no girls have joined yet. Early days, though, I s'pose. What's it like having an affair with the Environment's top pin-up?'

'Don't believe everything you read in the papers –'

'That's a bit political.'

'Norbert. Shut up. I –'

'How did you jump through that plate-glass window without hurting yourself?'

'Oh, I'm just magic, that's all.'

'Cripes! Where are you going?' Edward checked his watch.

'Home.'

'Great! I'll come with you. Now, what we need to get things going is a few of your personal things, you know: photos, knick-knacks, old biros, that sort of thing – so's we can start a collection of your most treasured items. For the Movement.'

Edward hailed a cab. To his relief it didn't recognize him.

He rolled into the back seat and pulled Norbert in after him. 'This Movement. Will it help defeat the AmJap Corporation?' he asked.

'Will it help?! I should cocoa!'

'Right. When we get back to my house, you can have all the knick-knacks you want. We'll see what we can find.'

'Great! That's brilliant! You can make me lunch and I can tell you all about it. What I had in mind was to produce a weekly fax sheet with news, views, quizzes, competitions, a personality profile, a lonely hearts column —'

Twenty minutes later the taxi came to a halt outside Number Thirty-Two, Bluff Cove Crescent. Norbert was still talking: '— and then, of course we can hold activities weekends and get to know each other and act out famous scenes from your past and —'

'Hi, Edward. Who's your friend?' said the doorbell. 'Listen, I wouldn't go in there if I were you. A coupla gooks called earlier and, and . . .'

'Well?'

'I can't tell you. I —'

'I'm Norbert. Hallo.'

'Hi, Norbert.'

'Oh, come on. Open up.'

'I'm warning you, Edward. It could be dangerous.'

'Norbert,' Edward said. 'They might have planted a bomb in there. Go in and check it out.'

'What? Oh. Yeah.' Edward handed him his keycard and stepped back. Norbert steadied the keycard over the lock. A small but powerful force-field seemed to have established itself over the slot. 'Ermmmmmmmmmmmmmmmmmm,' he said, 'I've just had an idea. It could actually be great for the Movement if you did get blown up, actually. Not for you personally maybe, but think of Elvis. Think of Margaret Thatcher. Think of the Busby Babes. Didn't do *them* any harm, did it? We'll build you a mausoleum. A sort of shrine. A focus for the Movement. Oh, go on. Please. It's your bloody house.'

'Oh, alright.' Edward snatched away the card, wiped the sweat off it on his pyjama trousers and opened the door. Norbert dashed to the end of the path and clutched a gatepost. 'I'll wait over here and marvel at your courage,' he shouted.

Edward walked into the dim hallway and gave a strangled cry. Trembling from head to foot, Norbert approached the open door. 'Oh, wow,' he said. 'It must be a booby-trap. I can't believe what's happening. I'm having an out-of-body experience. Wow. Life on the edge of danger! Edward! Edward! Call me a mad, crazy fool, but I'm coming in.'

In the hallway, Edward was sobbing over a heap of scrap household equipment. He peered over Edward's heaving shoulders and saw the fetcher, its insides trailing across the earthern floor like spaghetti, its display-lights emitting a faint and ghostly flicker. 'Cor,' Norbert said. 'Disembowelment. That's a very trendy way to do it.'

'The only machine I ever loved,' Edward blubbed.

'Give it a kick. Sometimes helps,' Norbert said, swinging a leg.

'Can't you see it's suffered enough?' Edward protested. Norbert deliverd a crisp kick into the fetcher's midriff and folded his arms. The fetcher stirred and let out a soft, tremulous crackle. 'Oh, Edward . . . Edward . . . Edward . . .' it moaned.

'Told you,' said Norbert.

'Fetcher . . . You're going to be all right,' said Edward.

'Am I?' the fetcher asked.

'I shouldn't think so,' said Norbert. 'There are bits of you everywhere.'

'Do you mind?' Edward blazed. 'Fetcher. Who did this to you?'

'I'm sorry about the mess, Edward.'

'Who was it?'

'It was . . .' Edward put his ear close to the fetcher's mouthpiece. 'It was . . . It was . . . meant for you.' There was a prolonged silence.

'You're wasting your breath,' Norbert snorted. 'It's dead. Suppose we'll have to make our *own* lunch now.'

Edward turned his face to the ceiling and cursed the AmJap Corporation.

'That'll make a great story for the newsletter,' Norbert interjected. '"*I Was There*, by Norbert Seriously." Where's the kitchen? I'm starving.'

The telephone rang. 'Are you going to answer that?' Norbert shouted from the kitchen. Edward passed on into the living room and picked up the receiver. For a moment he failed to recognize the beaming features on the screen.

'Edward. There you are. Why don't you ever answer your bloody phone?'

'Don't you realize the AmJap people are trying to kill me, Gordon?'

'Pass. Listen. I've just had the most productive lunch of my life. Take a look at my new office.' Gordon directed the handset around him. 'It's the trendiest office in my entire career. It's a perfect archetype of design for design's sake.'

'Where is this office, Gordon?'

'AmJap Headquarters. Colonel Brad and I have just managed to knock together the most amazing salvage plan for your image.'

'Gordon. Listen to me —'

'Hear me out, Edward. You may well see sense. AmJap and I have agreed that Edward Wilson should be promoted as Public Enemy Number One. And I'm talking Number *One*, not bubbling under. You're big, bad, mean and horrible. Believe me, it's a runner.'

'Gordon. You're fired.'

'Ha! Ha! Knew you'd say that! Hey, this place is amazing. Fantastic equipment, and some very, *very* exciting people. Now, you could be a part of this if you'll only let yourself.'

'There's only cheese. Do you want the one with piccalilli?' said Norbert, emerging from the kitchen with a leaky sandwich in each hand.

'Not now, Norbert.'

'Who's that, Edward?' said Gordon.

'Oh. Gordon. Meet Norbert. Tell him about the Movement, Norbert.' Norbert stuffed a whole sandwich into his mouth.

'Hallo. You want to join the Movement, then?'

'What's that?'

'A cheese sandwich. It's disgusting.'

'No. The Movement.'

'Oh, what? You've never heard of the Edward Wilson Movement?'

Gordon shifted in his leatherette recliner. 'Edward. Let me in on this,' he said. Norbert swallowed another mouthful of cheese and piccalilli and handed Edward the dripping remains.

'It's an underground personality cult. I'm surprised you didn't know about it. You're missing out. It's big, it's commercial, and membership is free to girls. Do you know any?'

'Look,' said Gordon, thumbing feverishly through his Filofax. 'Let's do lunch.'

'Sandwiches, or a proper hot one?'

'Oh, a hot one. Anything you like.'

Edward prized the handset out of Norbert's hand. 'Stay out of this, Gordon,' he ordered, shoving it back into its cradle.

'Whatya do that for?' said Norbert.

'Tactics,' Edward explained, taking a bite from Norbert's sandwich. 'Wait here. Gordon'll be round like a shot.'

'It's not safe here, Edward,' said a deep voice.

'Ah! Where'd he come from?' said Norbert, turning sharply.

'Don't worry, Norbert. This is Lunk. He's sworn to protect me. He's my blood-brother.'

'Got any sisters?' Norbert asked.

'Lunk,' said Edward. 'This is Norbert. You might find it hard, but try not to kill him.'

'Oh, ha ha . . . Thanks a lot,' said Norbert.

Lunk tilted his nose to the air and drew in a series of rapid sniffs. 'This house isn't safe for you, Edward. I smell danger,' he said.

'I know,' said Edward. 'They killed my fetcher here this morning.'

Lunk drew in another noseful. 'The male, short and oriental. The female, Calfornian with an M-16 rifle,' he announced.

'How do you know that?'

'Combat-trained,' Lunk said, tapping the side of his nose. 'Those people are out to kill you.' He took a clip from his belt, clapped it into his sub-machine gun and sprang over the window ledge. 'I'll follow my nose and sniff them out. Lie low where they can't find you. Good luck.' He merged suddenly and imperceptibly into the undergrowth.

Edward thought hard. 'Norbert,' he said finally. 'You stay here and wait for Gordon. I've just had an idea to help the Movement. Don't tell anyone where I'm going.'

'Why? Where are you going?'

'To see Tabafa Minx.'

'Wow! Do you think she'll join?'

'No harm in asking.'

'Blimey!' said Norbert. 'Tabafa Minx! Cor!'

46

'. . . forty-one, forty-two, forty-three . . .' Tabafa Minx was in her private gym pushing some tiny, fluffy weights. '. . . forty-nine, fifty . . .' Pink, cuddly toys and customized fluffy gadgets with cute smiles lay scattered among chrome-plated apparatus. '. . . sixty-seven, sixty-eight . . .' she gasped. Beads of sweat became rivulets on her face. Her stupendous bust rose and fell under her skimpy leotard. '. . . ninety-nine, a hundred! Phew!'

Physically, the exercises were a doddle. The hardest part for Tabafa was the counting. She lay back exhausted on her pink, padded funfur bench and lowered the weights to the carpet. Her father charged into the gym waving a video tape above his head. 'Have I got a lovely surprise for you,' he said.

'Oh, yeah. What have you done this time? Sold me into slavery?'

'Now, now, Tab. Bit of respect for yer ol' Da, if you don't mind. I've just just landed you the biggest, most exclusive contract you've ever had. Wiv the AmJap Corporation. Here it is.' He tossed the video cassette on to her perfect thighs.

'That's fantastic, Dad.'

'An' all for an undisclosed lump sum in advance.'

'What's an undisclosed sum, Dad?'

'Just legal mumbo-jumbo, my pretty little dumbelle. You just sign it and then you can have a look at it on the video later. It's an unusual contract. Very rigid and binding. They're going to keep you the number one pin-up girl forever.'

'How can they do that! I mean, we all get old one day.'

'Apparently not. Not under this contract, anyway.'

'What?'

'Don't worry about the legal mumbo-jumbo, lovey. Yer ol' man'll look after that. Just sign it on the label and Daddy'll be on his way.'

Tabafa inspected the video cassette, took a pen from her father's hand and signed the label. She peeled it off and passed it back. 'There y'are, Dad. Wanna cuppa tea?'

'Nuffink stronger?'

She danced to the drinks cupboard and poured him a large scotch. He downed it hastily and stuffed the bottle into his coat pocket. 'Well. I'd better be off,' he said, checking his watch. 'Ta-ra love. And keep taking the pills.'

'Awright, Dad. I won't forget. Bye!'

Tab heaved a sigh, slipped the video into the playback console, lay back in her pink, funfur hammock and watched. Brad appeared standing before a sombre backdrop of metallic blue. Tab surrendered to wild surmise about Brad's marital status. 'Hi Tab!' he said. 'Brad Matterhorn, Controller, AmJap Environment. You're gonna spearhead a campaign to put the Environment to work for the AmJap Corporation. I look forward to meeting you. There'll be a full demonstration in simple, audiovisual terms after a short musical break. Watch the moving dot, listen and relax.'

The music wafted over her. Gazing into the swirling colours on the screen, she felt herself being pulled gently into a deep, hypnotic lake with the texture of marshmallow and suffused in subtle shades of pink. She felt herself become weightless and drift into another dimension.

Many hours later she found herself waking from the deepest, most comforting sleep of her life. Blinking around at her room, she knew that the future lay with AmJap and that someone was knocking on her door. She slipped off her leotard, stepped over to the security screen and arranged a cheerful grin. 'Yes, who is it?' she trilled.

'Tabafa! It's me! Er, your Great Uncle Asparagus,' said a bearded face. 'Let me in!'

'Blimey,' she said, pressing the unlock button. The man entered hurriedly, shut the door and supported himself against it, breathing fast and staring wildly. ''Ere, 'ang on. I 'aven't got a Great Uncle Asparagus. And that beard, it's false.' She pointed at the offending item.

'Sorry to frighten you, Tab,' said the man, removing his beard. 'It's me. Edward. I'm a bit well-known, you know, and this place is crawling with security.' He shut his eyes. 'Ah. Yes. Tab! I want you to spearhead a movement against the AmJap Corporation. Will you do it? It's desperate.'

'Oh, dear. I am sorry,' she said, touching her lip. 'I'd love to help, especially since we've just had an affair, but I've just signed an exclusive contract with the AmJap Corporation.'

Edward clutched his brow. 'Oh, no, not you as well! My manager's just joined them. And they're trying to kill me. They killed my fetcher this morning . . .' His lip trembled.

'Edward. Look. I was just going to cook my supper —'

'All right, yes, I'm sorry. I'll go now,' he stammered, fumbling for the door handle.

'No. I didn't mean that. I mean, you must be hungry. Fancy something to eat?'

Edward's face brightened. He followed her naked bottom as it wiggled into the kitchen.

47

Edward leant across Tabafa's pink, funfur dinner table and held her pretty hand in his. '– and this is the funny bit,' he chuckled, '– so the accountant took the meringue back to the shop and said: "Get me five more like that one. My wife's loves them!" Ha! Ha!'

Tabafa fell off her chair and Edward helped her to get up. She settled her elbows on the table and gazed. Edward yielded to her huge, turquoise eyes as they tunnelled into his own. The clock bleeped eight.

'Great,' she said, her fingers diving into a carton on the table. 'We can eat the chocolate mints now.'

Edward ran his eyes over her exquisite body. 'Tab?' he asked.

'Yes?' she replied, delicately taking a second mint to her plump, red lips.

'Do you ever wear clothes?'

'What? You mean wet tee-shirts, fish-net bodystockings? That sort of thing?'

'No, I was thinking . . . Oh, never mind.'

'You're deep, aren't you?' she said.

'Oh, I wouldn't say that.'

'Oh, yes you are,' she insisted. 'You've got a *mind*. Me, I'm just a gag 'n' boob girl. Y'know. "Gor Blimey – I must be the Environment's top double-act! Ha! Ha!"'

'So, you do know you're being exploited, then?'

'You see! You *are* deep. Not like the others . . .'

'Others?'

'You must have read about them in the papers,' she said, taking a fifth mint.

'Tabafa. Have you ever had a *real* boyfriend?' She tossed her mountain of shimmering, red hair.

'Dad says I 'ave to keep me, er ... me distance so's I can marry a toff later on.'

'A toff?' Edward snorted. 'Have you ever actually seen a toff?'

'No. Apart from Lord Snooty.'

'Lord Snooty is a cartoon character.'

'Is 'e? Well, at least he's not married, is 'e?' She bit her lip and sighed. 'I s'pose I 'ave led a sheltered life. Let's go to bed.'

Edward's jaw dropped open.

'Come on if you're coming. I'm fed up with my Little Miss Madam image,' she said, taking his hand and leading him up the spiral staircase to her pink funfur bedroom.

48

Under a moonless sky, the AmJap Corporation's two top destruction agents were squatting in the dustbins outside Edward's flat. 'Let's go,' CL whispered. 'He's not coming home tonight.'

'No,' Bushido hissed. 'This time we stay.'

'We can always kill him tomorrow . . .'

'A samurai of the AmJap Corporation does not sleep until he has done something violent. That is his art.'

'For the last time, Bushido. Violence is not an art, it's a science. And scientifically speaking, there's not a hope in hell of killing Wilson if he's not here.'

'Violence is an art you will never understand, CL.'

'It's a science!'

'It's an art!'

'Science!'

'Art!'

Bushido stood up and hurled his dustbin lid at CL. A red-hot stream of lead spewed through the air, through the dustbins, through Bushido, through CL and across Edward's garden, snatching scraps of flesh on the way and scattering them across the azaleas.

'Violence isn't a science *or* an art,' Lunk lectured the steaming bodies. 'It's just a way of life.'

49

'So,' said Gordon, pouring the last of the second bottle of Chateau Lafitte into Norbert's glass and watching him down it in two gulps. 'Basically we're talking residuals on a megascale. Telephone numbers.'

'Pardon?'

'Tee-shirts, videos, designer membership cards, that sort of thing.'

A waiter rushed forward with a menu. Norbert scanned it and licked his lips. 'Oh, that, certainly, Gordon. Oh, yes. You not having anything? I never can resist Black Forest cake, can you? – Yes, please. I'll have two, please, and big dollop of cream, please – But we will have to bump up the female membership a bit. There aren't any girls in this Movement thing at all at the moment, to be brutally frank.'

'I'll use the facilities at AmJap,' said Gordon. 'We are gonna make Edward Wilson the biggest cult movement since sliced bread.'

50

Crichton thumped his tumbler on the desk. 'From now on I'll just have to make it all up,' he grunted. Facts had become even more scarce since Brown, his most valuable mole, had left for outer space.

He jerked his chair as close to the desk as his belly would allow, tucked a fresh, white sheet of A4 into the roller, twisted it through, squared it, reset the paper bail, twiddled his fingers, made final adjustments to his sitting position, coughed, drew a deep breath, cracked his knuckles, poised an index finger over the letter F, stared at the blank sheet and then straight through it. A mixture of lunch and Old AmJap Gin rose in his gorge. He refocused on the keys, clutched his temples and wept as he wrote:

Draft 894

I DID IT ANYWAY
THE LIFE AND CONQUESTS OF DRAKE MATTERHORN
CHAPTER THIRTEEN — THE ENVIRONMENT TAKEOVER

As his ultimate project neared completion, Drake Matterhorn, megaplutocrat and multizillionaire, diverted his energies into the provision of lavish entertainments for his two pulchritudinous twins, Jay and Natalie, at their home, the fabulous GoldTops in Pearl Harbor, Hawaii — the nucleus of the AmJap Corporation.

Drake's final project was the total enslavement of the Environment, a fiddlingly minor country formerly known as Britain. The task was being overseen by Drake's beloved brother, Colonel Brad Matterhorn, who had already built two thousand electric people-power stations within the Environment. Only one of the population, Edward Wilson, saw fit to delay this conclusion. God help the poor bugger.

Crichton yanked the sheet out of the roller and screwed it into a ball. There was a knock at his door. Brown entered wearing a battered spacesuit. 'Crichton,' he said. 'That's decided it. Don't ask me how, but we're getting out of here and we're going home if it's the last thing we do. That's if there's a home left to go to.'

'There isn't, I'm afraid.'

51

Two naked bodies lay entwined in Tabafa's pink funfur bed. For four days Edward and Tabafa had stretched the concept of sex to new boundaries. During that time they had been excited, frightened, amazed, shocked, frenzied, amazed again and finally exhausted.

At eight o'clock on the morning of the fifth day, Edward opened his eyes and wondered where he was. An alien alarm clock was telling him to get up and the roller blinds had shot open. It was as if several days worth of sunlight had burst from behind a dam. Just as Edward was remembering where he was, Tabafa sprang over him, off the bed and into the shower.

'Come back,' he said. 'I've got a surprise for you.'

'You get yourself some breakfast,' Tabafa shouted back from the bathroom. 'I'm in a hurry.'

'What?'

'I've already told you. I've got to go to the AmJap Corporation. I've signed a contract to work for them. Remember?'

Edward winced. 'But AmJap's an evil organization dedicated to destroying the Environment and killing me.'

'Is it?' She stepped out of the bathroom and started pillaging her wardrobe.

'That's why I'm hiding here, remember?'

'No. I mean, is it evil?' She held a dyed ostrich feather against her pubis and frowned into the mirror.

'Of course it's evil. What do you think attempted murder is? Naughty?'

'I'm not an intellectual. I don't pretend to understand politics.'

'So you're going to pose nude to help publicize an evil organization, is that it?'

'Almost nude, yes. You see, there's a moral principle involved. I've signed a contract.' Edward gripped the pillows.

'Tab. You can't go. I forbid it.'

Tabafa sat down at her pink funfur dressing-table and shook an aerosol. 'I'm not your property,' she pouted. 'I'm the sole property of the AmJap Corporation. It's in the contract. They own me, body and soul – in return for which I'm going to be the top pin-up for the rest of my life.' She sprayed glue on to her nipples and fanned them dry.

'You don't actually believe that, do you?' said Edward, rising on to his elbow. 'You can't *stay* young, you know.'

'Oh, yes I can. It's in the contract. I'm going to stay cheeky, chirpy and nineteen forever.'

'That's obscene!'

'I *knew* you'd like that bit,' she giggled, tapping a mother-of-pearl nipplecone into place and turning to face Edward. 'What d'you fink? These or the sequins?'

'I won't let you go!'

'I'm doing this for your sake,' she said, holding a heart-shaped stencil over her pubic mound and spraying it with glue, 'and if I don't go there now, someone from AmJap'll come and collect me.' She took a handful of pearls from a silver bucket and patted them into place. 'You don't want them to find you, do you?' she said, dripping a trail of pearls across the floor and down the stairs. She opened the door and stepped out into the hallway.

'Please don't go, Tabafa!' Edward called as the door clicked shut.

'You're safe now, Edward. She's gone,' said Lunk, heaving himself up from under the bed.

'How long have you been under there?'

'Since yesterday. Been out killing. Trying to forget.'

'Forget? Forget what?' Lunk shook his head.

'It's gone.' He tutted and stroked Edward's brow. ''Ere. You look rough. You've not been eating right. Chocolate and sugary nonsense, I should think. I've been listening. You don't chew enough. A hundred and thirty-six times you should, before you swallow. I'll rustle you up some proper breakfast.'

Edward watched his protector lope off into the kitchen. 'Television?' he said. A pink funfur box rose like a miniature Wurlitzer from the carpet.

'Yes?'

'Do some channel-hopping.'

'You're not going to like this.'

'Next on Channel Twenty-Seven,' said a presenter. 'Edward Wilson: an in-depth profile of the Environment's most hated man —' The screen hopped to a man-in-the-street archetype in front of a row of shops.

'Edward Wilson? The very thought of him makes me shudder, actually,' the man said. The television hopped again:

'And this is a tricky one for that fabulous Pacific Holiday. Who in nineteen eighty-nine was responsible for the South Shields Baby Massacre . . .?'

'BZZZZT Edward Wilson?'

'Correct!' Another hop, this time to a talking head with a leather-bound books backdrop: 'And we'll be previewing Gordon Blank's new book: *Edward Wilson, Complete Bendy Thing — Or Not?* after the break —'

'Okay, okay. That's enough.'

'Told you, didn't I?' the television said.

The door announced that someone was waiting outside in the hall.

'Who is it?' Edward shouted back.

'A sort of subhuman in surgical pyjamas,' the door answered.

'Let him in,' Edward sighed.

Norbert panted up the staircase and stood on the top step.

'Five bloody days ago you said you were just popping out to see if Tabafa Minx would join the Movement. What happened? Wasn't she in?' he said.

'Unfortunately she's just popped out to work for the AmJap Corporation.'

'Oh well . . .' Norbert ran his eyes along Tabafa's dressing-table. 'The Edward Wilson Movement's really going great, by the way, no thanks to you.' He stuffed a purple G-string into his pyjama pocket. 'You're extremely popular you know, all thanks to me.'

'Don't you ever watch television?' Norbert raised a finger.

'Ah. You're controversial, yes. But membership's just topped a million. Gordon's got it all on computer in his new office.'

'What?'

'Well, he's your manager, isn't he?'

'I fired him when he joined the AmJap Corporation.'

'Oh. Well,' Norbert shrugged, subjecting a sheer body stocking to close inspection and jamming it into his pocket. 'Gordon's not one to bear a grudge. He's working really hard for the Movement. Mind you, he's very busy. Apparently he's running some hate campaign or something as well. D'you think Tabafa will join us? Only there are rumblings among the membership about a shortage of the girly element.'

'Why don't you go back to the members and drive home the real message.'

'Message?'

'About the AmJap Corporation, you idiot. Can't you understand anything? Listen. What particular hate campaign do you think Gordon might be running? And who for? Think about it.'

'Dunno, really. Gordon's being a bit funny about that.'

'You're a moron, that's what you are.'

Norbert brushed some imaginary fluff off his chest. 'You haven't noticed, have you?' he said.

'What?'

'These. The new designer jimjams. Everyone in the Movement wears them now. Gordon bought the franchise. He even supplies hospitals now. Only the genuine originals have got this special label. Sexy, eh?'

'Fine. Just make sure you get the message across. Now, clear off!'

'Oh, right. Tata. I'll be off then.' Norbert waved and left.

'And don't tell anyone I'm here!' Edward called downstairs. 'Lunk!' Lunk kneeled at his side with a tray of food. 'Lunk. We've got to rescue Tabafa.'

'AmJap Environment HQ is a fortress. It's in the middle of the Thames.'

'I don't care. Whatever it takes.'

'I'll have to get some equipment. We'll row across in a disposable dingy, fire rocket-harpoons to the roof, climb up the ropes and abseil down the other side. Eat this.' He held out a plate. Edward recoiled.

'What is it?'

'Breakfast.'

'Looks disgusting.'

'It is. Good for you. Cracked wheat, mashed carrot and Pedigree Chum. It's what *I* eat. Feel that.' He pressed Edward's hand against his nose. It was cold and wet.

'I'd rather just have a bowl of Tabafa's Honey Puffs, if you don't mind.'

Lunk carried the bowl back to the kitchen. 'Girls are bad for you,' he muttered. 'A man should keep himself pure. My Dad told me my body was a temple . . .' He opened the fridge door and paused. 'Or was it a Friends' meeting house?'

52

Two spotty young men called Keith and Ian sat face to face across a table in one of the last remaining nineteen-eighties theme cafés in London. They were wearing identical, green surgical pyjamas. They gesticulated wildly when they spoke and frowned intermittently into their empty coffee cups.

An autoserver trundled to their table. 'Yes?' she asked, licking a pencil and pulling a grimy pad from her pinafore pocket.

'It's all right, thank you,' said Keith.

'You've bin 'ere 'alf an hour. You gonna eat anyfink or what?'

'Do you mind? We're waiting for somebody,' said Ian.

'Well, go home and get dressed.'

'You don't understand,' said Keith. 'This is the ideal *milieu* to sit in and discuss important issues.' The waitress stood her ground and sighed.

'Awright,' said Ian. 'We'll have a pot of tea and a slice of cheesecake.'

'That told her,' said Keith as the waitress trundled back to the kitchen. 'Now, Ian. It's time for me and you to talk about the forthcoming activities weekend for the Norwood branch of the Movement —'

Keith stopped to sigh at the tall, bronzed AmJap official with gleaming teeth who was standing over their table.

'Hi, there! Wanna get fit?' said the stranger.

'That seat's occupied,' said Ian.

'Mind if I join you?'

Keith looked doubtfully at the empty seat.

'Thanks. Say! You wanna get fit! Of course you do! Turn

that flab to AmJap muscle. Take these drugs. They *make* you fit.' He tapped a bottle of white pills on to the table top.

'Actually, we're in the Edward Wilson Movement,' Ian said, tossing the bottle back across the table. 'And we don't believe in AmJap stuff.'

'Course you do,' the man replied. 'Say, I bet you guys are hot with the girls, ha?' He elbowed Keith and winked. Keith laughed and nodded. 'See these?' He slapped a handful of glossy eight-by-tens on to the table. They were pictures of Tabafa Minx looking leaner, fitter and younger than ever before. Her grin was more inviting, her breasts firmer and higher than at any time in her career. She was pouting irresistibly on various complicated bits of gymnastic equipment.

Keith furrowed his brow. 'I thought Norbert said she was going to join us!' he said. The stranger shook his head and laughed.

'Like the uniform? They all wear that. Now Tabafa's a beautiful AmJap girl. Just look at that muscle tone. Like so many other of our delectable cuties, she's enjoying a new way of life with AmJap as a willing love-slave. And they're all dying to meet you.'

'Are they?' said Ian. Keith dived across the table and clutched his shoulders.

'Ian! It's a trap!' he shouted.

'— But they can't wait forever. Why not sign up now? Tomorrow you could be enjoying yourselves at one of our new activities camps,' the stranger continued, spreading two brightly-coloured application forms over the photographs. Ian snatched at Keith's top pocket for a pen. 'That's the AmJap spirit. Those lucky girls!' the stranger chuckled as Ian frantically administered the suck of life to Keith's pen.

'Well, Ian, if *you're* going to join . . .' Keith said.

At that moment, Norbert Seriously entered the café.

'This should be interesting,' said Ian.

'Hi, soldier. Wanna sign up to AmJap?' the stranger asked.

'No, thank you. Is that your armoured car outside?'

'Sure. Pretty neat, huh?'

'Only there's some kids fiddling with the aerial . . .'

The stranger shot out into the street.

'We certainly fooled him, didn't we, Keith?' said Ian as Norbert took the empty seat.

'Ha ha! Yes. We made him think we were going to sign up!' Keith laughed, waving the application forms at Norbert.

'Oh ye of little faith . . .' Norbert said, shaking his head. Keith and Ian fell silent. A full minute passed before Norbert spoke. 'Now, I want you chaps to listen patiently to what I have to say. As you've probably noticed, Tabafa Minx has agreed to pose temporarily as an AmJap girl. Now that doesn't mean to say −'

'She hasn't joined the Movement, has she?' said Keith.

'− *as* you promised.'

'She was abducted. I was there when it happened, actually − well, nearly. Now, I've just had some instructions from the very top, re AmJap bombings −' Ian tapped the photos with his forefinger.

'So, not wishing to change the subject, Norbert, e.g. the girly situation: how are we going to persuade any girls to join us, then, if we can't get Tabafa Minx to lead the way and make everyone think we're really sexy with these extremely expensive jimjams? You tell us that, Mr Smartarse.' He threw an injured look at Norbert. Norbert slapped his hands on the table.

'Look. Forget the girly element. There's no guarantee they'd talk to us even if they did join. First of all, we've got to clear Edward's name and expose the AmJap Corporation as evil. I have that on the highest authority.'

Ian and Keith exchanged a sceptical look and folded their arms. 'Sounds a bit political to me,' said Keith.

'Mmmm,' said Ian. 'I think the membership's got you by the

short and curlies over this one. We'll have to hold an emergency meeting about that.'

'One pot of tea, one slice of cheescake,' the waitress announced, banging the order on the table.

'Great!' said Norbert. 'Can we have three cups and three forks, please?'

53

'And this . . .' Colonel Brad Matterhorn said, making a sweeping gesture across the Central Control Room of the AmJap Environment Headquarters Buildings, '. . . is it!'

'Oh, I see. Yes,' said Tabafa.

'At ease, men!' A line of fifty uniformed agents executed a single, swift movement and stopped dead. 'Stand easy.' Another smooth movement. 'Stand difficult.' This time an impossibly painful position. 'Stand funny.' The line assumed an absurd posture and held it, eyes front and stony-faced. 'You see, Miss Minx. That's discipline. At ease! From this room we control everything. It all happens here.'

'Like what?'

'Wha, just about every durn thang thur is,' said Twang.

'Shut up, Twang.'

'Sawry, sur.'

'Well, Miss Minx, you've seen the whole building, now —'

An alarm sounded. The wallscreen flashed up the number 15000.

'Thar she blows, sur. That's the sixtieth successful explosion this morning.'

'Outstanding! I mean, how terrible! Damn those terrorists! *Damn!*' he wrapped a muscular arm around Tabafa's shoulders and guided her through automatic doors into a steel antechamber. 'Now, Miss Minx, I'd like you to try on this.' He held out a handful of green rubber.

'Whassat?'

'Working clothes, Miss Minx. Twang. Oil her, dress her and give her the drugs. An idle body is an abomination to the eye. Oil her good, Twang.'

'Yessir.' Twang slapped a slippery unguent on to her naked skin and wrestled her to the floor. He stretched the green, all-in-one, body-hugging, total-cover, see thru, rubber overgarment over her feet, up her thighs, around her bottom and up, over her head. He stretched the face-hole of the hood into position and teased the rubber over her arms and legs, aligning the fingers and toes into their sleeves until, finally, Tabafa was incarcerated from head to toe in watertight green. She staggered to her feet and planted her hands squeakily on her hips.

''Ow am I supposed to go for a pee in this lot?' she asked. Brad handed her a tiny bottle.

'You won't need to perform any of the less savoury human functions ever again. These drugs are all that goes in. Nothing comes out. You will have a pure body. One that is self-sufficient, efficient and environmentally non-pollutant. These drugs also convert flesh to muscle. Now that your body is ours, we're going to perfect it and use it to lure the people of this pathetic Environment into a lifetime of slavery.' Brad allowed himself a rare, contorted laugh.

'I don't understand.'

'All will be revealed, my pudgy little doughnut,' said Brad, prodding her down on to a steel chair. 'Twang, switch on the video.'

'AmJap and the Environment,' said a craggy face that filled a whole wall of the antechamber. Heavy, martial music boomed from the ceiling. The face melted away.

'People,' said another voice. There was a slow-motion tele-photo shot of thousands of people ambling over London Bridge. 'People are our main asset. The Environment has a population of seventy-five million, unfit, unmotivated, lack-lustre people. Our programme is to transform them. To create a bright, healthy population of willing slaves.'

'Here's a typical example,' said another voice. A slack-bodied, naked man stood against a plain background. He was picking his nose. 'Let's call him John Smith. Years of excessive leisure and petty decision-making have made him sluggish and unhappy.

'Now let's look at him as an AmJap slave,' the male voice said. John Smith reappeared looking like a sword-and-sorcery feature film hero. He flexed a mighty pair of pectorals. 'His eyes are bright, his cardiovascular system is A-1, he no longer suffers the problem of deciding what to do. He does what *we* tell him to. Jump, John!' With one bound, John Smith leapt clear out of shot. The picture flipped to the inside of a gigantic factory. John Smith entered dressed in studded leather straps and thongs. He clambered into one of the huge machines and began pumping his legs faster and faster, forcing the machine into motion. All the while he was smiling.

'Now he's on a treadmill,' said the female. 'He might have been a rickshaw-driver or a domestic servant, but happily the choice was not his. Soon John Smith will be joined by all of his compatriots in the Environment, working to make AmJap even richer.'

The martial music swelled as the picture encompassed the entire factory. Thousands of slaves were turning thousands of wheels and singing. It was the AmJap slave song. The picture faded.

'No-one'll put up with that,' said Tabafa.

'Happily they will, my little doughball. Slavery has acquired pejorative connotations in recent years,' Brad patted the top of her head, 'but that is merely liberal propaganda.'

'I don't want to be a slave.'

'There is always initial resistance to exciting new ideas. This can be overcome with the aid of modern science. Twang. Take her to the indoctrination room.'

Twang hauled Tabafa over his shoulder and carried her into the corridor. 'Go-lly. Are we gonna have ourselves some fun,' he chortled.

Brad watched Tabafa clawing at the reinforced steel door of the indoctrination room. 'Oh, Twang?' he called.

'Sir?'

'Come straight back after. It's nearly time for my electric shocks.'

54

One afternoon, Drake received the following memo from the Household Guards:

SURVEILLANCE REPORT 1269/C

ORIGIN OF OLFACTORY DISTURBANCE IN WEST WING POSITIVELY IDENTIFIED AS ASHLEY CRICHTON, ALCOHOLIC FAGGOT TYPE 47K, AGED 68, UNDER CONTRACT TO THE CORPORATION TO COMPILE BIOGRAPHY. AWAITING FURTHER ORDERS.

The idea of being written about struck Drake as a highly original and flattering notion. Though he had no memory of thinking up the idea in the first place, it was a stroke of genius and therefore attributable only to himself. He ordered that this writer be brought before him to be indoctrinated.

Dragged out of bed at eleven in the morning by two uniformed sadists while several other operatives stuffed his entire literary output of the last two years into bin liners, Crichton's first thought was that he'd finally died and was being taken up before God to account for his wasted life. He entered the Matterhorn nursery under armed escort. Trembling and sweating, he beheld his master for the first time.

'Read to me,' said Drake. 'Read what you've got so far . . .'

55

Mr Baines thumped the kitchen table with his fist. 'Keith. I don't want to hear another word about it. We are going to the AmJap camp in Wales today and you are coming with us.'

'No way,' said Keith. 'I've told you. No waysville.'

'We are not going to be the only family in the street that doesn't all go together.'

'We were the last ones to get megaglazing,' said Mrs Baines, carrying a frying pan over to the table. Dad held up his hand.

'Alright, love. Don't interrupt. I'm trying to reason with my son.'

'Forget it, Dad.'

'I'll kick your bloody head in if you don't come. We won't be eligible for the family prize. Where's my cup of tea?'

'In the pot,' said Mrs Baines, leaning her face close to the baby. 'Now, Craig. You want toast?'

'No!' Craig shouted, banging his spoon.

'I'll put it in the funny faces toaster . . .'

'Want the clown! Want the clown! Want the clown!' Craig shouted.

'Shuddup,' said Mr Baines, clouting Craig across the head.

'You'll never understand me, Dad,' said Keith.

'You'll understand the sharp end of my cutlass if you don't see reason,' said Mr Baines, shaking his fist.

'You've never let me express myself,' said Keith. 'Well, those days are over. I've joined the Movement.'

'Aw my Gawd!' said Mrs Baines, dropping a plate.

'Yes. The Edward Wilson Movement. Dedicated to the overthrow of the AmJap Imperialists.' Mr Baines gripped the sides of the table. Veins bulged on his temples.

'Mum. Go and get the cutlass!'

'You're not going to hurt him, are you?'

'Course I bloody am.' Mrs Baines left to fetch the cutlass. Keith clenched his fists under the table. Craig banged his spoon.

'Oh, that's typical, that is. Physical violence. Well, I'm twenty-three and technically that's an offence,' said Keith. The doorbell rang.

'Oh, no,' Mr Baines muttered under his breath. 'His boyfriend's arrived.'

'Ha, ha. Very funny, Dad.'

'Come in, love,' said Mrs Baines, ushering Ian into the kitchen and passing the cutlass to her husband. 'We're just having breakfast.' Ian grinned in the doorway and waved at Keith.

'Hello, Ian,' said Mr Baines. 'What's that I see? Is that a love-bite on your neck?'

'Oooooh, Ian!' Mrs Baines said, wagging her finger. Ian blushed and clutched his neck.

'What's going on?' said Keith.

'No,' Ian giggled. 'It's a spot. What are you doing with that cutlass, Mr Baines?'

'He likes to cut his toast with it,' Mrs Baines laughed, miming the action.

'Oh. You coming, then, Keith? We're supposed to be at a meeting. We'd better get there early or we'll be late.'

Mr Baines fixed his eyes on his son. 'I'm sorry, Ian, but Keith's coming on holdiay with us today. We're going to an AmJap camp.'

'What! You told me you weren't going. Can I come, Mr Baines?'

'Course you can, Ian. There's plenty of room. There's a special train. It's going to be great. There's even a song we're going to sing. How's it go, Mum?'

'Er . . . Oggi oggi oggi . . .'

'Oi! Oi! Oi!' said Craig, banging his spoon.

'Good boy,' said Mr Baines. 'Have my bacon rinds.'

'Oi! Oi! Oi!' said Craig, banging his spoon.

'All right, Craig.'

'Oi! Oi! Oi! Oi! Oi! Oi! Oi! Oi! Oi!'

'Shuddup.'

'I've got bad news for you,' said Keith, standing up. 'I'm leaving with Ian to follow Edward Wilson.'

'What? That murderer? That evil enemy of the Environment?'

'That's AmJap propaganda!'

'Oh, I see. So we're all idiots, are we? But it doesn't fool you, is that it?'

'Just try to understand, Dad. It's something I've got to do.'

'Get out of my sight, you big sissy. You're no son of mine!'

'Right!' Keith stuck his chest out and walked to the door. 'Come on, Ian. We're going. Bye, Mum. Goodbye, Mr Baines.'

56

'"Drake Matterhorn listened intently to his biographer as he read aloud in the nursery, and suddenly stopped ..." That's it, Mr Matterhorn.' Crichton eased his weight from one foot to the other and back again. He had stood and read fifteen bin liners full of discarded drafts. Drake eyed him suspiciously.

'You sure you're the greatest living author?'

'Oh, absoutely, sir. The best money can buy.'

'Good. God knows I must have paid you enough. So? Is there any more? What happens next?'

'With respect, sir, there cannot be any more for the time being. What happens next is largely up to you now, Mr Matterhorn. The biography is bang up to date at this point. You see, you do the things first, sir, and then I write them down.'

Drake smiled. 'Okay, Crichton,' he said. 'So we pick it up from here, do we?'

'Yes, sir.'

'Okay. So where was I? Read me that last part again.'

'Er . . . Blah blah blah etc. etc. etc. Drake Matterhorn listened intently to his biographer as he read aloud in the nursery, and suddenly . . ."'

'Okay. I'm with you! Brown!' Brown glided in through the door.

'Sir?'

'Where are my sublimely beautiful children?'

'I'll call them, sir.'

'Okay, Crichton, get some more in like the part where I discovered the cure for cancer and scored a million home runs for the New York Giants. I never heard that before. Is it true?'

'In vino veritas, Mr Matterhorn'.

'Pardon me?'

'I need a drink.'

'I need you to stay here and write down everything I do, so's you can read the last bit back to me whenever I lose my thread. Okay?'

'Er, okay.'

'Okay!'

Uniformed attendants brought Crichton a mobile recliner, portable word-processing equipment, some large bottles of Old AmJap Gin and a packet of Woodbines. He set to work immediately as Jay scrambled through Brown's legs and rushed to his father.

'Daddy! Daddy!'

'Happy birthday, son. How's that little country I gave you to play with?'

'Oh, Daddy. I goofed. I changed the climate and the crops failed and all the little people starved . . .'

'Hey! It doesn't matter.'

'You're just saying that, Daddy.'

'Listen. I didn't have a country of my own to play with until I was twenty and I wiped it out in a war.'

'Daddy! You're so funny! I love you!' Jay hugged his father's craggy neck.

Thundering into the nursery and dressed in street gear, Natalie let out a piercing shriek and hit the power button of a ghetto blaster the size of an upright piano. 'Daddy! Daddy! Watch me! I can breakdance!'

'Natalie, my sylph-like daughter!' Drake cried, as tears sprang from his eyes.

'Watch me!' she bellowed.

Brother and father watched as Natalie destroyed most of the costly toys and electronic equipment that lay scattered around the nursery. Finally, she collapsed into her father's arms.

'Natalie, you are the most talented dancer in the world,' Drake crooned, patting her fat back. 'Now, children, as today is your birthdays I have a special announcement to make.'

'What is it?' Jay asked, turning his oversized blue eyes to his father.

'Your Mummy has left home forever.'

'Oh, Daddy. I miss her,' said Natalie. Drake stroked her hair.

'It was because Daddy found out Mummy's awful secret.'

Jay clenched his little fists. 'Was she cheating on you, Daddy?'

'In a way, son, yes. She was cheating on all of us. You see . . . your Mummy was . . . old.'

The twins cowered and gagged. Drake passed them thick handfuls of money and the crisis passed. He told them to close their eyes for a big surprise and then to open them. They did as their father asked. In the nursery doorway stood a beautiful young woman.

'Hello, darlings,' she said. 'I've heard so much about you. I just know we're gonna be friends.' She drew them close and kissed them.

'I love you, Mummy,' Natalie gasped.

'So do I!' said Jay. 'She's *perfect*!'

'Say,' said the new mother, chucking Jay under the chin, 'I've got today all figured out. We're gonna have fun!'

The children cheered and ran out into the grounds with their brand-new Mummy. Drake picked a hand mike from the air and Brad appeared on a bank of monitors along the wall. 'Hi! You look fantastic. How's the Environment?' he said.

'Almost done,' said Brad. 'All power stations are now operational. Slaves are enrolling at a rate of one hundred thousand per day.'

'That's fantastic. How'dyo do it?'

'Hold on to your seat,' said Brad. He held up a video cassette and slid it into his console. Tabafa Minx in her green, see-thru body-condom splashed into view, dancing to a sumptuous beat and licking her top teeth. 'Hello,' she purred. 'You know who I am, don't you? If you wanna get to know me better, you'd better do what I do. I work for the AmJap Corporation.' She jiggled herself closer to the camera and performed the Naughty Schoolgirl look that first launched her page and screen career. 'Fancy working with me?' she asked.

Drake raised a shaggy eyebrow. 'Looks great.' He turned to watch the children outside. 'Say, Brad. Gotta go, now. It's the kids' birthdays.'

Brad slapped his forehead. 'Aw, gee, I'm sorry. I forgot.'

'That's okay. Don't worry. They got another one tomorrow.'

'Great. I'll send something over. If I can find anything left that's worth having.'

57

Brad dialled an internal number. An office appeared on his screen. Gordon Blank emerged from within the folds of a leather upholstered office swivel chair. 'Hi Brad,' he said, re-settling his glasses.

'It's *Colonel* Brad, creep!'

'Sure.'

'Gordon, you're doin' a great job on the hate campaign,' Brad barked.

'Thanks, Colonel Bradcreep.'

'Let me square with you.'

'Why not? See who salutes it.'

'I'm putting you in the driving seat, Gordon.'

'Well, let's bounce it around a bit and see where it ends up.'

'How's it feel?'

'From where I'm standing, the headline looks good.'

'Is that an affirmative?'

'Colonel Bradcreep. I'm up the wall and steaming.'

'Good. That's settled.'

'I don't quite catch your drift . . .'

'Gordon, as of this moment there is a new head of the Slave Recruitment Campaign.'

'Really? Who's that?'

'You, you moron.'

'Fan-bloody-tastic!'

58

Gordon let go of his desk and slid back into his chair with a sigh. The intercom buzzed. One of Gordon's three receptionists announced that Norbert Seriously was on the line yet again and would Gordon please take the call this time, as he was becoming a bit of a pest. Gordon hauled himself back up towards his desk.

'Hi, Norb. How's the Move?'

'Well, we have lost a few members to the AmJap Corporation, but membership is now approaching two million.'

'Are you still shifting the surgical jimjams?'

'Yeah. Do you think we could have them designed a bit sexier? Only –'

'Still no girls, eh? Bad luck.'

'Yeah. I think there's going to be a rebellion about that unless we act fast and neutralize the ringleaders. I'll give you a list of names if you let me take one of your receptionists out to the pictures. How about it? Deal?'

'Sure. Heard anything about Edward?'

'Wow! I'll take the blonde one. Yes, two things. One, I've *seen* him in Tabafa's flat, and two, on the news, several reliable eyewitnesses saw him on the street with the Leopard, carrying ropes, a rubber dingy, climbing equipment, all sorts of stuff. Armed to the back teeth, apparently. Warnings not to approach either. What's her name, this receptionist, then?'

'Typical of him. Just when the Movement's taking off he goes on holiday. He's irresponsible, that boy. Selina, I think. Can't talk now, Norbert. Someone's just come in through the window.'

The entire glass wall on one side of the mile-high building shattered and cascaded into the Thames. Edward and Lunk stood facing Gordon. 'Hi,' he said. 'Thought you two were going on holiday together. Just got back?'

'Shut up, Gordon,' Edward spat. He rammed Gordon against a wall and pinned him there. 'Where's Tabafa?'

Lunk banged a clip into his Kalashnikov and aimed it. 'Let's kill him first and then ask the questions,' he growled.

'Let's do lunch,' said Gordon.

'*Where is she?*'

'Are you serious?'

'Yes.'

'Good. I hate jokes like this.'

'Where's Tabafa?'

'I don't know. She's on the work programme somewhere. I'll have to ask the Database.' A panel in the wall behind Gordon's head lit up.

'Yes?' it asked. 'What is it?'

'Gimme a fix on Minx, Tabafa.'

'*Please . . .*'

'Yes, just tell me where she is! I've got a gun against my head.'

'I don't care where it's pointed. Manners don't cost anything.'

'All right. *Please.*'

'She's in generator unit two, level four, zone seven, area six, sector twelve, and I'm not repeating it.'

'Right,' said Gordon, straightening his tie and easing Lunk's grip. 'I think you got that. See you later. I'll stay here and grow old and fat.'

Lunk stepped back and gestured to the door with his gun. 'You're coming with us,' he commanded. 'We'll need you to get us past security.' Gordon managed a grin.

'Edward. Can I just say what a pleasure it is to represent you again?'

'No, you can't,' said Edward, dragging him through the door.

59

'You two wait out here,' Edward said to Gordon and Lunk as he eased open the armoured door. Inside was a lavishly equipped gymnasium. Each free-standing exercise machine had an electronic dashboard that was connected to a network of electric cables. At the far end of the room, Tabafa was running inside a huge, plastic wheel, her muscles tautly defined under her transparent, green rubber skin. 'Hi! It's me!' Edward called, bounding towards her. 'I've come to rescue you.'

'Oh. Hallo Edward,' Tabafa smiled. 'I knew you'd join up in the end. Nice, innit?'

'I hardly recognized you.'

'Yeah. I'm all muscle now.' She pounded the treads and glanced at a dial.

'Come on. We haven't got much time. What are you doing?'

'I'm working. I'm a happy slave and this is my treadmill. Great, innit?'

'Wonderful. Now, come on. We've got to get out of here.'

'Yeah. It's brilliant. All the difficult jobs are going to be done by robots and computers. We just make electricity.'

'What?'

'People power! People are the most efficient renewable energy source there is. We're all going to run round in huge big wheels and push bars and pull levers to make electricity for the AmJap Corporation. We get all the fun and fitness and they get the electricity.'

'I can't believe this.'

'You're just suffering from initial resistance. They've got a machine that cures that.' Edward glanced at the door.

175

'Tab, I don't care why you're doing this –'

'Oh, that's the best bit! For these.' She pointed to a dispenser on the dashboard. Out popped a white tablet. Tabafa caught it in her mouth and swallowed.

'Pills?'

'Yeah! The harder you work the more you get. They're absolutely packed with vitamins and drugs to make you happy, fit and healthy. Oh, and I really *am* going to be nineteen forever, by the way!'

'We've got to stop them before it's too late!'

'*Plus* I've got special responsibilities. Look.' She selected a button on the dashboard. On the monitor, Edward could see a colossal hall filled with wheels, exercise bicycles, weights, benches, ropes, pulleys, levers and thousands of muscular men and women in green rubber outfits, all smiling and pumping in the same, dull rhythm. 'Chop-chop, busy-busy, work-work, bang-bang, chop-chop, busy-busy, work-work, bang-bang,' they chanted.

'That's power station sixty,' Tabafa explained. A remote boom camera swung down from the ceiling. She upped her pace to sprint speed and puckered. 'Hello, boys and girls!' she panted, waving to the camera. On the screen the slaves turned to their monitors and waved back. 'It's Tabby here! You're all doing terribly well!'

'Hooray!' the workforce cheered, doubling their pace. 'Hooray! Chop-chop, busy-busy, work-work, bang-bang. Chop-chop, busy-busy, work-work, bang-bang!'

Edward kicked the brake lever, caught her as she toppled forward, grabbed a handful of squeaky rubber at the scruff of her neck and heaved her, kicking and screaming, out into the corridor.

60

Peeled of her green, rubber skin and dangling by the ankles from the picture-rail of Norbert's bedsit in Dunstable, Tabafa pleaded and sulked for three days while Edward maintained a constant vigil. 'Your young lady's still got cold turkey, I notice then,' said Mrs Wigge, Norbert's landlady, as she thrust a plate under Edward's nose. 'A little more ham?'

'Cut me down and let me work!' Tabafa groaned. Edward shook his head.

'I'm doing this for you, Tab. I love you.'

'Liar!'

'Now, now. Cup of tea, love?' said Mrs Wigge.

'Naff off!'

'Ooooh. And to think she's the Environment's top pin-up,' said Mrs Wigge, clutching her breast and retreating behind her hostess trolley. 'Well, it's nice to hear young people's voices in the house again, anyway. Norbert didn't have *any* friends until recently. Twelve years he's been living under my roof. I thought I knew all his little habits, but he's changed so much recently I feel I hardly know him at all. He hasn't touched his Scalextric for weeks . . .'

'Yes. Strange, isn't it?' Edward sighed.

'There's an Airfix Lancaster been lying unfinished on his desk since last Wednesday. And he used to *love* rambling, though I never used to listen. Oh, *dear*. Should she be that colour?'

Tabafa had turned bright yellow. 'Aw!' she said, blinking at Norbert's room. 'I think I'm back to normal now.'

'Ooh, that's lovely. You can't put a price on sanity, can

you?' said Mrs Wigge. 'Would you like to try one of my cold cuts?'

Edward held Tabafa's inverted face and peered into her eyes. 'Fancy a spot of work? Running on a treadmill? Lifting things?' he asked.

'Do us a favour.'

'How about a pill?'

'How about cutting me down?'

Edward gave the thumbs-up to Mrs Wigge. 'It's all right. I think the crisis is over,' he said. He slipped the knot and lowered Tabafa to the carpet, then knelt forward and kissed her. Mrs Wigge wiped away a tear with her pinny. There was a knock at the door.

'Hallo, gang. Can I come in?'

'It's your room,' said Edward, carrying Tabafa to the sofa.

'I know that, but I could see you and Tabafa doing things through the keyhole,' Norbert said, opening the door.

'Norbert Seriously, you're a very rude boy,' said Mrs Wigge.

'Knickers. I'm thirty-five, I'm in charge of five million people and I can say what I like!'

'You tell Auntie Wiggie where you've been,' she scolded, removing his surgeon's cap.

'Oh, it was great. I organized a mass rally and —'

'Did you underline the message?' Edward interrupted.

'What message?'

'The message to save the Environment from total subjugation. That message. Remember it?'

'Well. We had a meeting about that proposal and the majority of the members feel it's a bit political.'

'Of course it's political! The Movement's a political organization!' Edward exploded. Mrs Wigge held her hand to her mouth.

'Language, Mr Wilson, please!'

'That's only *one* view,' Norbert smirked. 'I think that in any democratic organization the views of the majority should hold sway, and the majority of the members in this particular case feel that the main aims of the Movement are the camaraderie, the clothes and the overall style of the thing.'

'And that's *it* for you, is it?'

'There is the search for a meaningful relationship, but since no girls have joined, we've had to play down that aspect of late.'

Edward stood up. 'You're pathetic!' he bellowed. 'I put my life in danger for this cause and now you tell me all the Movement's concerned with is faffing around at rallies, comparing surgical pyjamas and trying to find a girlfriend!'

'Well, you've got one!' Norbert protested, pointing at Tabafa. 'And a *nice* one!'

'That's it,' Edward exploded. 'Why should I bother with five million nerds who think that avoiding enforced slavery is politically contentious!?'

Norbert turned bright red. 'Right, that does it!' he screamed at the top of his voice. 'I've worked hard for this Movement. I've organized rallies, I've sold surgical pyjamas, I haven't *touched* my Scalectrix for weeks! But that's not good enough for Edward Wilson. Oh, no. We all have to have exactly the same ideological viewpoint as him. Well, let me tell you, Mister Edward bloody Wilson, you can stuff it!' He tore off an 'I love Edward' badge, threw it on to the floor, stamped on it and burst into tears. Mrs Wigge pulled at the cords holding up his surgical pyjamas.

'He's over-tired,' she explained. 'Come on, Norbert. Let's get your proper pyjamas on and put you to bed.'

'Shut up, Mrs Wigge!' Norbert sobbed, stamping his other foot. Mrs Wigge held out his pyjama bottoms for him to step into.

'Auntie Wiggie knows best,' she said. 'You mustn't blame Norbert, Edward. It's not his fault.'

'It's Gordon Blank you should blame,' Norbert sniffed as Mrs Wigge tucked him into bed. 'He's been managing the Movement.'

Edward stepped out into the hall and picked up the handset of the wall telephone. 'Oh, hi, Edward,' said Gordon. 'Great news. The surgical pyjamas are going like hot potatoes.'

'Listen to me,' Edward began through clenched teeth. 'As my personal manager —'

'Ah-ah-ah! Please. Your personal marketing representative.'

'— I think you should know I've had it with your promises. I'm finished risking my life for the Movement. I'm leaving the country,' Edward shouted. Gordon's face crumbled.

'Don't do that to me, Edward,' he said.

'To *you*?! What about *me*?'

'Now, don't go all ego on me, Edward. You're not the only big organization in the Environment that needs my services.'

'No. There's the AmJap Corporation, isn't there?'

'Professional etiquette, Edward. I couldn't possibly disclose the identity of another client.'

'You're fired.'

'Let's have lunch over this. I've got some very hot ideas and I *know* I can persuade you you're wrong.'

'How?'

'Don't worry. I'll think of something.'

Edward exhaled heavily. 'All right,' he said. 'We'll meet here for lunch tomorrow at Norbert's flat.'

'Fabby.'

61

'Twain! Twain! Twain!' said Craig, pointing at the brightly-painted intercity liner.

'Shuddup,' said Mr Baines, slapping Craig on the head and pulling him up the step into the corridor.

'Welcome aboard,' the hostess smiled, making a tick on her clipboard. 'We have four seats reserved for you.'

'Yeah. Well, there's only three of us, actually. One of us got ill at the last minute. Our son, Keith.'

'Fine,' said the hostess. 'We don't want unhealthy ones. Now, we've organized a little game. Nothing sinister. We just wanna have a laugh, don't we?'

'Not half,' said Mr Baines.

'Goody. Okay. Now, the menfolk are gonna have fun in the rear portion of the train; the ladies are gonna have fun in the middle portion, and the kiddies are gonna have a fun medical examination at the front of the train.'

Mrs Baines looked at Craig doubtfully. 'Is that necessary?' she asked.

'The video is running and there's a complimentary bar at the rear, sir.'

'Don't make a fuss, dear. Sounds very nice,' said Mr Baines.

'That's the AmJap spirit,' the hostess beamed, handing him a fat, plastic envelope. 'Don't forget your Fun Pack.'

'What's in it?'

'Drugs to make you happy.'

'Bloody great,' Mr Baines said, snatching it and heading for the bar. 'See you later, love. Bye bye, Craig.'

'You come with me,' said a nurse, leading Mrs Baines by

the arm. 'Oh my, Mrs Baines, what good muscle tone you have. It's carriage "B" for you.'

'Hallo,' said another nurse, crouching low and smiling at Craig. 'You're a pretty big fella for a three-year-old. Do you know your blood group?'

62

There was a bleep at Gordon's office door. He squared his shoulders and planted his elbows on his desk. 'Come in,' he called. The door hissed to one side. Brad Matterhorn stood in the doorway. 'Hi, Brad,' Gordon said, swinging his feet onto his desk.

'It's *Colonel* Brad, scum! At ease, men.' Several heels thudded into the carpet outside.

'Who are your friends, Colonel Bradscombe?' Gordon asked.

'My elite killers.'

Gordon rocked back in his recliner and raised a hand. 'I'm getting a bad feeling here,' he said. Brad pointed at Gordon's telephone.

'Who have you been talking to?' he asked. Gordon gulped and scratched the end of his nose.

'My mother.'

Brad spoke into his wristwatch. Gordon's wallscreen burst into life to show a split-screen telephone conversation. Gordon sucked some air between his teeth.

'Now, listen, Gordon,' Edward was saying on the left of the picture. 'The Movement will fight AmJap to the last man, but we need your solid support.'

'Don't worry,' said Gordon on the right. 'I'm one hundred per cent behind you.'

Brad snapped his fingers. The picture froze.

'That's uncanny,' Gordon said, staring wide-eyed at the screen. 'That guy looks and sounds just like me.'

Brad stood in the doorway, legs apart, arms folded. 'That

guy has been doing bad things against the Slavery Programme, Gordon.'

'I hate him more than you do, Colonel Bradscombe. What a nerve, impersonating good old Gordon Blank, trustworthy head of the AmJap Slavery Programme, faithful, loyal . . . and . . .'

'You have betrayed my trust, Gordon.'

Gordon placed his hand on his heart. 'Colonel Bradscombe. I cannot tell a lie — it wasn't me.'

'Men,' Brad said after a long pause. 'Begin the demonstration.'

The men marched in carrying a table and a large watermelon. On the table was an industrial-size kitchen blender. 'Observe closely, Gordon.' Brad said. 'I'd say the melon was about the size of your head, wouldn't you? Begin.' The watermelon was lowered into the blender, the lid sealed. One of the men turned a knob. Violent, tearing sounds erupted from the blender. Gordon covered his ears and eyes until the noise stopped. He peeped through his fingers at the table. On it stood the watermelon. 'Biotechnology from AmJap,' said Brad. 'The watermelon's eaten the blender — and unless you start telling me some names and addresses, you're next!'

'Colonel Bradscombe,' Gordon began. 'I couldn't possibly disclose the identity of another client.'

'Okay, Gordon,' Brad shrugged. 'Men!'

Gordon watched the men carry the melon towards him. 'Colonel Bradscombe, I'd *love* to tell you,' he said. 'So I will. I'll lead you directly to Wilson so's you can nail him for good.'

'There's a good boy.'

63

'Another wedge of kweesh, Mr Blank?' Mrs Wigge said in her poshest voice. Gordon took a slice.

'Thanks. I must say, what a lovely spread,' he said, taking her hand and looking into her eyes. 'And what a charming little hostess, too.'

'I've got to hand it to you, Gordon,' Edward said. 'You're a genius at something or other.'

Gordon drained his teacup. 'I have to admit, it was one of my better ideas,' he said. 'It should make everyone happy, which, if you ask me, is what the job of life is all about. Have faith. It will work. There are five million guys in the Movement and they just need motivating, that's all.'

'But I still don't understand. You agree to meet all my demands in return . . .?'

''S'right.'

'. . . to represent no other cause but the Edward Wilson Movement?'

'Yup.'

'I still don't understand —'

'That's the beauty of it, Edward. Trust me.'

'Could you pass me one of those, please?' said Tabafa, pointing at a mountain of chocolate logs at the far end of the table. Norbert grabbed them and dived across the table, landing the plate in front of her. Mrs Wigge hauled him back to his seat and slapped his wrists. 'You'll have to watch him, Tabafa,' she said. 'I think he's taken quite a shine to you.' Norbert blushed and hid his face in his hands.

'No no no no! Shut up. Rubbish. It's not true!' he shouted.

'I should hope not. Girls destroy your manhood,' said a

deep voice from the window. Norbert, Edward, Tabafa, Mrs Wigge and Gordon turned. Lunk, swathed in guns, ammunition, knives and grenades loped down from the ledge. With lips pursed, Mrs Wigge went to the cupboard for an extra placemat.

'You're supposed to be my bodyguard. Where have you been?' Edward said.

'Been out on reconnaissance.'

'Find anything?' Edward asked.

'Yeah,' said Lunk, banging a clip into his Kalashnikov. 'Two tanks and four hundred heavily-armed AmJap soldiers.' Gordon raised an eyebrow.

'Oh?' he said. 'Whereabouts?'

'Just outside.'

Edward leapt out of his seat. 'What?'

'Don't worry,' Gordon sang, rocking back in his chair and holding up a glistening palm. 'That'll be the arrestogram. It's all part of the plan. Trust me, Lunky Baby. The arrestogram people are expecting you. It's a publicity stunt.'

'But you didn't say they were going to be AmJap people, though, did you?' said Edward.

'Didn't I? No. No, I didn't. That was the big surprise until Matey here blew the gaff. They're *disguised* as AmJap officers to add authenticity to the stunt. Imagine the headline news tomorrow morning: "Wilson Arrested By AmJap Thugs". There'll be mass sympathy all round and no more of that Public Enemy Number One nonsense. The Edward Wilson Movement can start campaigning for AmJap to release you and everyone'll be happy all round. Look, I thought I explained all this.'

The door to Norbert's room came crashing inwards, along with the surrounding wall. An armoured truck appeared from the clouds of choking dust, pointing a heavy gun at Edward's head. A troop of infantrymen charged in on either side and poised to attack. A hatch opened in the roof of the vehicle.

'Nobody move,' Colonel Brad Matterhorn shouted, emerging in full dress uniform.

'I hope that tank doesn't mark my carpet, young man,' said Mrs Wigge.

'Shuddup,' Brad snapped.

'Nice one, Brad,' said Gordon.

'It's *Colonel* Brad, bum!'

'Cup of tea, Colonel Bradbum?' Mrs Wigge asked, laying out some extra placemats.

'Obliterate that woman,' Brad ordered.

There was a short burst of automatic fire. Mrs Wigge fell twitching to the floor. 'Nice cup of tea. Nice cup of tea. Nice cup of tea. Nice cup of tea. Nice cup of tea. Nice cup of tea. Nice cup of tea. Nice cup of tea. Nice cup of tea. Nice cup of tea,' she said. Smoke rose in thin wisps from her ears and a tangle of wires splayed out from under her shredded pinafore. Norbert's mouth dropped open.

'Blimey!' he said. 'All these years and I never realized my landlady was an android!'

'You didn't think female stereotypes like that existed in real life, did you?' said Tabafa. 'Oh, how extraordinary. I appear to have regained my intellectual faculties at last.'

'Tabafa Minx,' Brad roared. 'You're a traitor. Edward Wilson, you're under arrest. Norbert Seriously, you're pathetic. You're all coming back to AmJap Headquarters.' Gordon nudged Edward in the ribs and winked. 'You can't say this isn't convincing, can you?' he said.

'Okay Gordon,' said Brad. 'You've earned your reprieve. Now shut up.'

Edward turned to face Gordon.

'Judas!' he whispered.

'I can understand you thinking that,' Gordon replied. 'But what I cannot accept is your recriminatory attitude. I am therefore left with no choice but to tender my resignation, operative forthwith.'

Edward looked to Lunk, but Lunk was gone. 'Arrest the prisoners,' Brad commanded. Edward, Norbert and Tabafa were dragged to a waiting vehicle.

'This arrestogram's fantastic. It's just like the real thing,' Norbert said as they hauled him across the rubble.

'It *is* the real thing, you cretin. We're doomed,' Edward muttered.

'You may take us, but the Movement lives on!' Norbert shouted, shaking his fist at a line of news cameras on the kerbside.

64

In a dark thicket somewhere near Orpington, the Leopard sat waiting for the moon to rise. 'I love you Edward,' he said, stropping his blade against his belt. 'I will continue your fight. Alone again. Naturally.'

65

Twang read aloud from his screen: 'All but five million of the Environment are now AmJap slaves. Those five million are all members of the Edward Wilson Movement.'

'That's a lot of surgical pyjamas,' said Brad.

'No, sir! It's true! Oh, an' we got Tabafa Minx and Norbert Seriously caged, Gordon Blank in his new office, Wilson prepared for interrogation and your brother on line six.'

'Put him through and wheel Wilson in.'

Twang snapped a salute, pressed a button at his console and turned. Drake Matterhorn burst onto the wallscreen. 'Drake. You look fantastic. How's old Pearl Harbor?'

'Fantastic. How's the Environment?'

'In twenty-four hours, we'll have reduced the entire population to blind, drug-crazed, idiotic, AmJap slaves.'

'I'm proud of you. You've served the Corporation well. Be home by the weekend, the kids miss you.'

'Did they get their birthday presents?'

'I knew there was something important. Natalie was thrilled with the ballet company. She had them do Swan Lake. I didn't figure out the story, but they thrashed around in this big lake until they all drowned. It was moving.'

'How did Jay like the Red Arrows?'

'Flew them into a mountain.'

'Any survivors?'

'Jay was too upset to look. You must meet my new wife when you get home.'

'How is she?'

'On paper she's great but we haven't really put her through the hoops yet. Hey. Gotta run. It's the kids' birthdays.'

'Shoot. There isn't anything valuable left over here to send them.' The steel doors hissed open. 'Say. I've got to put some electrodes on some guy's tongue right now. But don't worry. I'll think of something. So long.'

Twang marched through the door with Edward strapped to a steel wheelchair. Two crocodile clips were clamped to Edward's tongue, a wire attached to each clip. 'Behold,' Brad said, carrying the ends of the wires over to a car battery. 'This can turn over a quarter ton internal combustion engine at one hundred and twenty ar-pee-em. No need to imagine what it can do to your tonsils, because –'

He touched the wires to the terminals. Edward jerked and convulsed as his tongue swelled to resemble a large fillet steak. The spasms subsided. 'Remove the clips and give him a shot of shrink,' Brad ordered. Twang jabbed a hypodermic into Edward's tongue, which immediately shrank back to normal size. 'There,' Brad said. 'It removes the swelling, but not the pain. Now, Wilson. You gonna be a slave or a corpse?'

'You'll never make me a slave!' Edward croaked. Brad's eyes flared.

'I hoped you'd say that. How would you like your ashes? Scattered over water, or in an urn? Because ashes are what you're gonna be. This,' he said, reaching for a long pole. 'is connected to a people-power generator – four thousand pairs of happy feet are at this very moment pounding the treadmills of Battersea to create a nerve-zapping two hundred and fifty thousand watts. Just for you. Yum yum yum.'

'If you kill me, the Movement will rise up and destroy your Slavery Programme!'

Brad lowered his face into Edward's. 'You and I both know the Movement is a joke,' he sneered. 'I'll just put this on,' – he pulled an arc-welder's mask over his face – 'because it's blammo when you go up. Twang, activate the prod.' Twang leapt to the switch.

'Okay,' Edward said. 'What do you want from me? I'll do it, whatever it is.'

'Now, where do you want it? The left nipple is the quickest, so we won't go there . . .'

'Please! Anything!'

'Stop wasting my time. I've got that worthless marshmallow Tabafa Minx to toast next,' Brad sneered. Edward jerked himself erect.

'Kill her and you'll regret it, Matterhorn!' he bellowed.

'Feelings, eh? You primitives are so pathetic. Hang on to your eyebrows, because –' He poised the prod over Edward's nose.

'If you harm her, they'll turn against you. I've only got five million followers but she's got the whole Environment. She's got charisma, you see. It's a rare gift –'

'A gift . . .?' Brad's eyes narrowed. 'Twang!'

'Yessir?'

'De-activate the prod. Mr Wilson has broken my heart with his pathetic display of bravado.'

'What? It's not a trick, is it?'

'No, Mr Wilson. You are a brave, intelligent and wise man. I have decided to spare your life. However, the AmJap Corporation cannot risk your continued presence in the Environment. You are so powerful, you could smash us.'

'I could?'

'So you must go away. Say, Hawaii? AmJap will provide you with a beautiful house, staff to surround you and great people to be with.'

'On one condition, Colonel Matterhorn.'

'What?'

'That you won't kill Tabafa.'

'A brilliant idea. She can go with you. You drive a hard bargain, Mr Wilson. It's a deal?'

'Bloody right, it is.'

'Fine. We'll fix you up a stratocruiser and get you there as fast as possible. I'm on a tight schedule. Twang. Release Mr Wilson here and uncage Miss Minx.'

66

'The world is not what it was, Crichton, and never will be,' said Brown. 'Would that it were. I miss the old country. Great Britain. Remember that? I miss the good old days. The eighties. Remember Mrs T? *Minder* on the telly? Those little supermarkets? We really had never had it so good, you know, and never since. I say, wake up old boy. Don't waste the only civilized company for several thousand miles.'

'Sorry, Brown, old chap. Do you know how many hours of sleep that bastard lets me have per day? Just under two. He never bloody stops. I have to be there to record every bloody detail of his pointless life. I tell you, he's killing me faster than the gin. And he's barking mad, of course. Power has corroded his brain. He genuinely believes he can do anything that chances to slop into his head. Memory like a sieve, too. I have to keep reading the last bit of the biography back to him to remind him where he is. Not only had to remind him what his new wife's name was last night, but what he was doing to her at the time. Do you know? Next time he asks me what he's up to I've a good mind to make up any old daft nonsense just to see him pick it up from there.'

'I say, Crichton,' said Brown. 'I think you might be on to something.'

67

As night descended on the woods somewhere near Orpington, a lone psychopath stirred his billycan as it bubbled over the fire. The smell of pine cone and woodlouse stew drifted towards Petts Wood. He howled at the moon. An AmJap stratocruiser glided silently across it.

He checked his watch and turned on his field television. 'The Movement,' said the solemn newsreader. 'was founded on Wilson's belief in hard work, AmJap justice and the inalienable right of the individual to surrender himself to slavery. After his tragic suicide pact with Tabafa Minx, the Movement acted swiftly to appoint a new leader. We interviewed him in his fabulous, new office.'

'Gordon,' the interviewer began. 'As leader of the Movement, what of the future?'

'Ah ah ah,' Gordon corrected. 'Not leader, no. More like General Director of Policy Co-ordination. The future. Well, coming up, we've got a very exciting new designer range of rubber pyjamas and a very exciting merger with the AmJap Corporation.'

Next came a shot of Norbert Seriously astride an exercise bicycle. 'But what does this tragic death mean for the ordinary members? The General Secretary of the Edward Wilson Movement told us.'

'Well,' said Norbert. 'Edward was obviously a factor in the Movement. It was, after all, founded on him. He did contribute quite a bit to it. But one mustn't overestimate his importance. Image is really what really matters today, and of course the weekly coffee break for members to get together for a quick chat and to swap items of memorabilia before getting back to the treadmill.'

'Meanwhile, George Minx has been mourning the loss of his daughter, the famous pin-up Tabafa Minx.'

George was plodding in his treadmill. 'What a waste eh? What a terrible waste,' he said. 'I set her up real nice and what does she do? She leaves her old Dad — me, an ol' man in the twilight of his life, who only cared about her investments — leaves me for this Wilson geezer. You know what I think? He poisoned her mind. And now she's dead.'

'In the vast Matterhorn Bioenergy Stadium in London, where the power of competitive sport is harnessed for the good of the national grid, a mass-rally was held within hours of the announcement of Wilson's death. Miraculously, all five million members of the Movement were there. Gordon Blank was the first to speak . . .'

'Members of the Movement. I am proud to be your new Figurehead-in-Chief. Good to see you all wearing the new rubber 'jamas. Believe me, it would have been what Edward would have wanted. I'd like to introduce to you now a man whose guidance I know the Movement is going to rely on in the exciting future ahead. Colonel Brad Matterhorn!'

Brad stepped up to the mike. 'Brothers! Shape up! Edward Wilson was a friend of mine. He was also one hell of a guy. You know why? He worked, he struggled, he never gave up. Remember that. He was a slave to his dream and today you can *be* that dream. You too can live in happiness, turning the power-wheels for this great Environment and for the AmJap Corporation. Join the AmJap Corporation and *be* somebody!'

'And that,' the newsreader concluded, 'is the essence of the Edward Wilson message.'

68

'Well,' Edward said as he opened the limo door for Tabafa. 'Here it is. Colonel Matterhorn really has done us proud.' Tabafa clapped her hands in wonderment at their new home. On the lawn by the gravel drive stood a small gathering.

'And look,' she said. 'The staff have assembled to greet us. Come on. Let's go and say hallo.' The welcoming party was singing in a little circle around two children.

> *Happy birthdays to you,*
> *Happy birthdays to you,*
> *Happy birthdays dear Jay and Natalie*
> *Happy birthdays to you.*

A tall man in butler's livery smiled benignly and turned to the tanned old man next to him. 'Mr Matterhorn, sir,' he said. 'The children's birthday presents have arrived.'

'Thank you, Brown,' the old man replied. 'Jay, Natalie!'

'Yes, Daddy?'

'Look what your Uncle Brad has sent you from the Environment for your birthdays. Aren't they neat?'

'What are they, Daddy?'

'Why, they're living dolls. They're yours to do with whatever you want.'

The children skipped over and prodded them with their fingers. 'That's swell, Dad,' the boy said. 'The male is just what I need for my Mars mission.'

'And she's so cute,' the girl squawked. 'I can dress her up and do her hair real pretty. I can play nurse and she can be real sick.'

'Could someone tell me what is going on?' Edward asked.

'Brown,' the boy shrieked. 'This toy is talking to me.'

'Don't worry, young sir. I'll deal with it. Toys! This way, please.' He led them away. 'Welcome to the toy-cupboard,' Brown said out of the corner of his mouth. 'How would you like to be the King and Queen of England?'

69

'You've done a great job, Brad,' said Drake, slapping his brother on the back.

'I did my doody for AmJap, Drake. That's all,' Brad replied.

There was a long silence. 'Shit,' said Drake. 'Where was I?'

Blearily, Crichton looked up from his screen. He exchanged a look with Brown. Almost imperceptibly, Brown gave a slow, encouraging nod. Crichton's heart threatened to jump out of its cage as he chose his words. 'Erm. "You've done a great job, Brad," said Drake, slapping his brother heartily on the back. "For your next mission I want you to go back."'

'That it?'

'Yessir.'

'Any idea why?'

'You were saying yesterday, sir, that you would like myself, Brown, Wilson and Miss Minx to sail back to the Environment on a luxury cruiser with Colonel Matterhorn and restore the Environment to its time of glory — the nineteen-eighties, sir.'

'You sure about that?'

'Oh yes, sir. I've got it written down.'

'Astounding. You got that, Brad?'

'Yessir!'

His eyes blazing, Brad snapped a crisp salute and marched to the rocket pad to begin his next mission.

From the bestselling authors of FOOTFALL

THE LEGACY OF HEOROT

LARRY NIVEN, JERRY POURNELLE AND STEVEN BARNES

Civilisation on Earth was rich, comfortable – and overcrowded. Millions applied for the voyage but only the best were chosen to settle on Tau Ceti Four. The Colony was a success. The silver rivers and golden fields of Camelot overflowed with food and sport nurtured by the colonists' eco-sensitive hands. It was an idyll, the stuff of dreams.

Just one man, Cadmann Weyland, insisted on perimeter defences: electric fence, minefield, barbed wire. Against what? Surely humans are the most destructive creatures in the universe? Surely the planet is friendly? Surely it's safe to walk in the fields after dark?

And beyond the perimeter the nightmare began to chatter . . .

'A version of ALIENS by writers who know the difference between Hollywood science fiction and the Real Stuff'
TIME OUT

Also by Niven and Pournelle:
FOOTFALL

By Larry Niven:
RINGWORLD
INCONSTANT MOON

0 7221 6407 8   SCIENCE FICTION   £3.50

OFFICERS'
ladies

MARION HARRIS

Confidence, beauty and privilege were advantages
Lieutenant Kate Russell took for granted. Her aristocratic
parents had great plans for her: when the war was over she
would marry a man with a pedigree as sound as her own.

Then she met Robert Campbell, a mere staff driver. And
her family would only accept their marriage if Robert
climbed the ranks of the army. But when peace is declared
and Robert achieves the rank of Major, Kate finds she has
her own bitter and personal war to contend with. Trapped
by her parents' possessive demands, tormented by Robert's
passionate but wayward love, she fights her own lonely
battle to save her marriage and her reputation . . .

Also by Marion Harris in Sphere Books:
SOLDIERS' WIVES

0 7221 4876 3   GENERAL FICTION   £2.99

The awesome spirits of chaos approach
their appointed hour . . .

THE

Time Raiders

BERNARD KING

The second in a trilogy of masterful invention

27 July AD 869. There was something unnatural, ungodly
about the rag-draped skeleton. The weathered white frame
appeared intact, if fallen in, but the skull was missing . . .

30 April last year. His face was like parchment stretched
across a skull which was no longer his own. His eyes, blue
and too young for his wrinkled, gaunt visage, smiled down
at those scrambling away in their panic before him . . .

The immortal forces of Thule insinuate their warring
passions through time, feeding the flame of mankind's
destiny. And as the shadows lengthen, the powers of
darkness thrill to the fulfilment of their deadly quest. But
their ritual is incomplete and they must steal the ancient
talisman from those who uphold the flickering light –
wherever and who ever they may be . . .

0 7221 4868 2   FANTASY   £3.50

Also by Bernard King in Sphere Books:
THE DESTROYING ANGEL

THE VISIONARY CHRONICLE OF THE ULTIMATE STRUGGLE TO RULE THE EARTH . . .

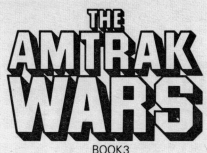

BOOK 3
Iron Master

The third volume of a futureworld epic

PATRICK TILLEY

The year: 2990 AD. The centuries-old conflict between the hi-tech underground world of the Trackers and the primitive, surface-dwelling Mutes continues with unabated ferocity. Steve Brickman, a Tracker wingman whose heart and mind is torn between the two cultures, embarks upon his most dangerous mission yet: the rescue of Cadillac and Clearwater, two Plainfolk Mutes held captive by the mysterious Iron Masters. It is a nightmare journey into the unknown . . .

0 7221 8518 9   GENERAL FICTION £3.50

Sphere Books 437 Proof 1 10.2.87 Opus Lazer 25649 F48 File 21

From the bestselling authors of
LUCIFER'S HAMMER and THE MOTE IN GOD'S EYE –
the ultimate novel of alien invasion!

FOOTFALL

NIVEN & POURNELLE

It was big all right, far bigger than any craft any
human had seen. Now it was heading for Earth.

The best brains in the business reckoned that any
spacecraft nearing the end of its journey would just
have to be friendly.

But they were wrong! Catastrophically wrong!

The most successful collaborative team in the history
of science fiction has combined again to produce a
devastating and totally convincing novel of alien
invasion.

FOOTFALL – the ultimate disaster

GENERAL FICTION   0 7221 6339 8   £3.95

The classic Amber series continues

ROGER ZELAZNY
TRUMPS OF DOOM

RETURN TO AMBER – The irresistible powers of the
kingdom beyond imagination draw Merlin, son of
Corwin, back to the magical realm . . .

Merlin is content to bide the time when he will activate
his superhuman strength and genius and claim his
birthright.

But that time arrives all too soon when the terrible
forces of evil drive him mercilessly from Earth, and upon
reaching Amber, he finds the domain in awesome,
bloody contention.

And in every strange darkness of his fantastic crusade,
there stalks a figure determined to destroy Merlin and
wipe out the wondrous world of Amber . . .

SCIENCE FICTION   0 7221 9410 2   £2.50

Also by Roger Zelazny in Sphere Science Fiction:

From the Hugo and Nebula award-winning author

TIME
PATROLMAN
by POUL ANDERSON

DEFENDER OF THE PAST . . .

The creaking Phoenician ship slowly approached its destination. Everard gazed out over the sparkling water at the ancient port of Tyre. "A grand sight indeed," he murmured to the captain, glad of the easy electrocram method of learning the language. His gaze went forward again; the city reminded him not a little of New York.

Time patrolmen like Everard guard the past. No matter how good or evil an event, it must be held inviolate. The slightest slip, and Time would become Chaos, and all that has ever been or will ever be will tumble into darkness. When the Birth of Civilization is endangered by the malign counter-emperor Varagan, the patrol must be on its mettle . . .

SCIENCE FICTION   0 7221 1290 4   £2.50

Also by Poul Anderson in Sphere Books:

interzone

SCIENCE FICTION AND FANTASY

Quarterly   £1.95

- *Interzone* is the only British magazine specializing in SF and new fantastic writing. We have published:

BRIAN ALDISS	GARRY KILWORTH
J.G. BALLARD	DAVID LANGFORD
BARRINGTON BAYLEY	MICHAEL MOORCOCK
GREGORY BENFORD	RACHEL POLLACK
MICHAEL BISHOP	KEITH ROBERTS
RAMSEY CAMPBELL	GEOFF RYMAN
ANGELA CARTER	JOSEPHINE SAXTON
RICHARD COWPER	JOHN SHIRLEY
JOHN CROWLEY	JOHN SLADEK
PHILIP K. DICK	BRIAN STABLEFORD
THOMAS M. DISCH	BRUCE STERLING
MARY GENTLE	IAN WATSON
WILLIAM GIBSON	CHERRY WILDER
M. JOHN HARRISON	GENE WOLFE

- *Interzone* has also published many excellent new writers; graphics by **JIM BURNS, ROGER DEAN, IAN MILLER** and others; book reviews, news, etc.

- *Interzone* is available from specialist SF shops, or by subscription. For four issues, send £7.50 (outside UK, £8.50) to : **124 Osborne Road, Brighton BN1 6LU, UK.** Single copies: £1.95 inc p&p.

- American subscribers may send $13 ($16 if you want delivery by air mail) to our British address, above. All cheques should be made payable to *Interzone*.

- "No other magazine in Britain is publishing science fiction at all, let alone fiction of this quality." *Times Literary Supplement*

- -

To: **interzone** 124 Osborne Road, Brighton, BN1 6LU, UK.

Please send me four issues of *Interzone,* beginning with the current issue. I enclose a cheque/p.o. for £7.50 (outside UK, £8.50; US subscribers, $13 or $16 air), made payable to *Interzone*.

Name _____

Address _____

_____

A selection of bestsellers from Sphere

FICTION

THE LEGACY OF HEOROT	Niven/Pournelle/Barnes	£3.50 ☐
THE PHYSICIAN	Noah Gordon	£3.99 ☐
INFIDELITIES	Freda Bright	£3.99 ☐
THE GREAT ALONE	Janet Dailey	£3.99 ☐
THE PANIC OF '89	Paul Erdman	£3.50 ☐

FILM AND TV TIE-IN

BLACK FOREST CLINIC	Peter Heim	£2.99 ☐
INTIMATE CONTACT	Jacqueline Osborne	£2.50 ☐
BEST OF BRITISH	Maurice Sellar	£8.95 ☐
SEX WITH PAULA YATES	Paula Yates	£2.95 ☐
RAW DEAL	Walter Wager	£2.50 ☐

NON-FICTION

FISH	Robyn Wilson	£2.50 ☐
THE SACRED VIRGIN AND THE HOLY WHORE	Anthony Harris	£3.50 ☐
THE DARKNESS IS LIGHT ENOUGH	Chris Ferris	£4.50 ☐
TREVOR HOWARD: A GENTLEMAN AND A PLAYER	Vivienne Knight	£3.50 ☐
INVISIBLE ARMIES	Stephen Segaller	£4.99 ☐

All Sphere books are available at your local bookshop or newsagent, or can be order direct from the publisher. Just tick the titles you want and fill in the form below.

Name _____

Address _____

_____

Write to Sphere Books, Cash Sales Department, P.O. Box 11, Falmou Cornwall TR10 9EN

Please enclose a cheque or postal order to the value of the cover price plus:

UK: 60p for the first book, 25p for the second book and 15p for each additio book ordered to a maximum charge of £1.90.

OVERSEAS & EIRE: £1.25 for the first book, 75p for the second book and 2 for each subsequent title ordered.

BFPO: 60p for the first book, 25p for the second book plus 15p per copy for next 7 books, thereafter 9p per book.

Sphere Books reserve the right to show new retail prices on covers which may differ fr those previously advertised in the text elsewhere, and to increase postal rates accordance with the P.O.